THE PASSION OF THE IMMORTALS

Maxime Norrvik

DREAMWICKS

To Shanna Smith

Acknowledgments

My thanks to Shanna Smith for her understanding about my work and for making this book possible, and to my daughter Sephil, whose smile drives me forward.

Let us go hence: the night is now at hand;
The day is overworn, the birds all flown;
And we have reaped the crops the gods have sown;
Despair and death; deep darkness o'er the land,
Broods like an owl; we cannot understand
Laughter or tears, for we have only known Surpassing vanity: vain things
alone Have driven our perverse and aimless band.
Let us go hence, somewhither strange and cold,
To Hollow Lands where just men and unjust Find end of labour, where's
rest for the old, Freedom to all from love and fear and lust. Twine our torn
hands! O pray the earth enfold Our life-sick hearts and turn them into dust
.

"Last Word." Ernest Dowson

1

A stone chamber with two chairs and a lantern on the floor. Antonio stares through the crying window at the unshakeable rose in the little garden plot—a silent, red heroine standing tall against wind and rain. The broken tombstone on which she stands shows her birthplace. She is so young, so red, so fertile. She is almost too large for a rose, as if the dead had been feeding her. Antonio stares, contemplatively, seemingly in awe of the sturdiness and resilience of that daughter of nature, who comes back every year almost to be eternal, like himself.

The chair next to his is empty, and around him is a carpet of leaves that has grown through the years.

Now and then he looks at Anika, his eternal companion, who wanders back and forth from the empty chair and fans herself with an old, white, hand-held fan.

Of a moment, Anika pauses to observe him, then looks at the fan in her gloved hand like she might like to turn it into a pan. She is displeased. She's a little angry beauty in a fabulous red Edwardian gown, one from ages past, the one in which she was buried—not in a grave, but in a tomb.

"The rain dampens all scent," Antonio says, as if that will mitigate Anika's sudden little glare. "Even for a corpse like me."

He has blue eyes, dark hair and fair skin, a combination of Spanish and German.

Anika gives him an unhappy look. "Maybe we should have gone out. We only come out once a week. Perhaps we should have stayed below."

Antonio turns to her. "Why? You would not want to ruin your make-up or that pretty dress. Besides, there is no moonlight below. When my dead eyes open, I understand the reason mortal men stay away."

"Since when do the dead care about wet clothes!" Anika responds. Both her hands go up. "Also, although dead, I know there are women in the world." She fans herself again.

"And braver than the men!" Antonio says. "Yet none as beautiful as you."

Though dead, Anika is a woman, and she blushes red.

A man of ambiguous race, though with a good stomach for one like him, appears out of the wide, open trapdoor on the floor. The thin dark skin over his bones is missing in places and reveals his skeletal parts, and his large blue eyes, round like marble, seem sunk in between his bony sockets.

Antonio greets him with a high wave. "Hey, Engusanado!"

Engusanado pauses, reflectively. "My name used to be Arthur. Though Engusanado is a proper name for one like me, considering all the worms in this here belly, though they seem to go nowhere. Yet Arthur used to be my name, I remember well. Death did not bury my memory."

Anika is peevish. She's adjusting one of her gloves. "It doesn't bury hunger, either!"

Engusanado pauses again. "I would give you blood if I had blood to give. Death took away my veins."

Anika turns to Antonio. "*He* would give me of his veins." Then turns to Engusanado. "*He* would close them over a little rain!"

Engusanado looks at Antonio. "A little rain scares the great dead? Do stones hurt one another? Maybe if one comes with fire and the other stone holds a column or a wall. But the stone doesn't scream."

Anika fans herself again. "I believe Antonio is the wall today."

"A lass well fed is a happy lass," Engusanado says. "That's the wisdom of the dead."

Antonio almost laughs. "Wise Engusanado, being a romantic, I've been protecting her beauty. Is that such a shame?"

"Beauty does not last on empty stomachs—or on empty veins," Engusanado says, a logical finger waving at Antonio.

"Aye, that's the wisdom of the dead!" Anika says, lifting her chin and fanning it.

Antonio gets up with a sigh. "Very well." He approaches Anika and holds her. "What is a little rain, indeed? I've just been waiting for it to ease a bit to help my scent, and to make mortals more at ease to step outdoors."

"I thought you were protecting my beauty," Anika says, raising playful eyebrows at him.

Antonio smiles, wryly. "My mouth can lie with words. Yet never with a kiss." He kisses Anika. "Your beauty can never be dampened, my love."

"Your mouth tells beautiful lies, just as it tells beautiful truths," Anika replies in good humor. "Quite the hearth, dangerous for one like me." She fans herself again. "But from now on, I won't know what is a lie and what is a truth, if your mouth is so rudder-less."

"Trust my immortal love," Antonio says.

"That is easy to trust, especially after I'm fed."

They look at each other a moment. Then, without even saying anything to Engusanado, they hold each other by the hand and run to the door.

Engusanado himself steps out of the mausoleum, though his walk is slow. By the time he steps outside, Antonio and Anika are gone. With bare, thinly-skinned bony feet, he bends over the wet garden floor and paws into the dirt. After much digging, he finds a worm, picks it up, and puts it in his mouth.

Around him are graves from the seventeen and eighteen-hundredth. The time-eaten tombstones and broken crosses no longer have any visitors. The old visitors were buried long ago, and the new generations no longer feel any attachment to the grounds. The cemetery is old and small, and decorated with an aged garden, where weeds and trees vie with the roses that have managed to stay alive.

He is back an hour later. Antonio and Anika are sitting on the chairs, licking their fingers.

"It was so delicious!" Anika says. A drop of blood is on her cheek. She cleans it up with her finger and puts it in her mouth. "There is life in the veins. It brings color to my lips. The mystery is solved as to why I am still beautiful and alive. Blood is life. It is color. If you had it once in a while, Engusanado, perhaps it would give meat to your bones."

Engusanado faces them, sitting on the floor. "I eat worms," he says. "They too have life, but give no meat to my bones."

"Then you ought to try something richer."

Engusanado waves his hands "I stay away from children. I am a kind corpse."

"Kindness kills during famine," Anika says. "But we do not kill children. They're too young to be flying about, and their blood is not very palatable. I insist, they're putting something in their porridge!" She turns suddenly to Antonio. They have discussed this before.

"But I have worms," Engusanado says. "And how can the dead die? We only suffer when awake. Famine won't kill us."

"True, but it weakens *us* against a stake, which can end all our prospects of ever coming out again, and enjoying death."

2

He's coming for seconds. The thirst for revenge is deeper than the hunger for blood, even if it ends in the same.

"My lovely child, where are you?"

She hides behind the bush lining the wall of an abandoned house. The open gate, through which she came in, gives view of the sidewalk.

"I can smell you," he says. But he can't smell her. He looks left and right. Nothing. He walks away. The street is silent, dark. Ravens fly and caw overhead. Except for them, all is quiet.

He doesn't go far. He steps to the side of a tree as if to hide. Twenty-minutes go by in absolute silence. After that time, without hearing or seeing anything, she feels more comfortable, though such a feeling is not retired from fear. She begins to make her away slowly out of the bushes. She stays low, pausing still to hear. Nothing. She looks beyond the gate. Just a little dash across to the other side and she might be safe. She gets out of the gate. She's so wary, she doesn't dash immediately. The moment she begins to take her steps, he stops her.

He claps his hand to her mouth.

She starts to cry. To panic. "Oh, no, not me!"

"Don't force me to kill you," he says. He forces her into a Model T parked on the street.

An hour later in an old, roadside inn, she is dancing for him in scanty clothes, and lying down on the bed. He makes her kiss him at the point of a dagger, makes her pretend she is enjoying it.

The next morning, the charlady comes in to clean the room. She finds her on the bed. The sheets are drenched in blood.

It is revealed she is from an important family in New York. She is rushed to the nearest hospital. Despite the blood transfusion and other treatments, the doctors don't expect much. She remains comatose. She is closely observed for two days, but she never wakes up. After the observation period, the doctors sadly pronounce her dead.

Only two days later, the book of her life is closed. Embalming is forsworn—the family wants a quick burial to begin the grieving process, lest the girl's mother loses what is left of her functioning mind. The mother cries at the funeral: "Find the man who did this!"

Her daughter was so young. So beautiful. So innocent. She is laid to rest in a stone casket, two feet above ground over a granite bier, five feet from an old cousin who died nearly a century ago. Other than the oils on her that replaced the embalming, she does not yet exude the smell of decomposition. On her is the long red gown that she had loved in life. She's also wearing gloves, and there is a ring on her ring finger.

The chamber is an elegant, family crypt under an old mausoleum, which still can be found today in a cemetery with an old garden.

The casket is closed. Life retires to leave the dead behind.

But she isn't dead. She wakes up half an hour later gasping for breath. She knocks on the lid above her, crying, "Let me out!"

She pushes up. The lid is made of lead and is too heavy to lift.

There is someone not far away from her. It is a man. Her cousin. He hears the knocks. The desperation. But he doesn't know what to do. He has respect for the crying dead. Some hours go by. When silence returns, he steps over to her casket, grabs a handle, and lifts up lid with ease. Anika has gone into a coma again. He looks at her in wonder, almost with love.

"So beautiful. Oh, so young! What happened to you? Did life bring you here to die, or was that the last cry of the dead? If the former, it is too late. Hmm...you cheek is getting cold. Too bad. You will die soon, my lady. Unless..."

He begins to think. He is greedy for companionship, and can kill two birds with one stone. Or with one bite. "Saving you from final death is to give me a friend," he says. He does the only thing that can stop final death. He bites her neck. He drinks much from her.

She doesn't come to for a while. As he inspects her, he notices the ring on her ring finger.

"Married? Engaged?" he asks.

He slides the ring off her finger and looks at it. There is a small inscription on the inner band. "William?" he says. "Interesting." He looks at her. "You won't need this. Reminders such as this are no good when a new life begins, even in death." He puts the ring in his breast pocket.

That was ninety-nine years ago.

Now Anika gets up every week during the night, pushing up the lid—the Newman Brothers hinges almost supernaturally still holding steady—and goes around to look for blood.

"Indeed, it is hard to enjoy life when one is dead," Engusanado says. "At least for me."

"Maybe you should get out a little more," Anika says. "That is what brings me happiness."

"Oh, I am not like you," Engusanado replies. "I have no wings. I got a slow step. I am different. A zombie as they say. I have no blood drop to give that could give them to me."

"I would be honored to give you wings, old man," Antonio says.

Engusanado is surprised. "Old man, me? I guess I am now. But I didn't die old. No, not me. I am still forty years old!"

"How come you died so young?" Anika asks. "Were you killed?"

"Me?" Engusanado goes into deep reflection. "I was poisoned."

"Poisoned!" Anika and Antonio are stunned. They have never before talked about Engusanado's death.

"Yes…eh…what year is it today?"

"Last I looked at a newspaper, two-thousand and ten," Antonio answers.

"Two-thousand and ten! That means I've been dead twenty years."

Antonio and Anika look at each other.

"She is fifty-five, likely still alive. Living off my fortune. Yes, yes. Well, I wish her happiness."

"You're a kind soul, Engusanado," Anika says. "When I found my killer, I made him do obscenities with a cow. Then I took him to the zoo, where the lions are. I would not turn him. He didn't deserve that."

"We are different souls," Engusanado says. "I wish my love happiness. I wonder if she still lives at the old house?" He is quiet for a moment. "Anyway, I've had my worms. It's time for my old frame to rest again."

Engusanado retires, going down the steps under the open trapdoor. The crypt is large, made to resemble the tomb of Romeo and Juliette. There are stone coffins around. Engusanado finds his open grave near the caskets of Antonio and Anika. It's not a big hole, which means it was dug quickly. He lies in the hole that is his bed and turns to sleep. Later, Anika and Antonio will throw the earth he removed on coming out back on top of him. They always try to cover him completely because they have affection for him.

Once Engusanado is gone, Antonio takes Anika in his arms and kisses her. They don't' care if Engusanado sees them or hears them. It is only an accident that they find themselves alone now. They have made love near his grave about the time he comes out. His hand pushes through the dirt very theatrically, a thing he likes to do to pretend he's a "scary zombie," and sits to watch them. They made love once in full view of spectators on the sidewalk, because their shame is gone. When the police arrived, they ran, and then disappeared.

Anika wasn't always like this. Back in the days of her mortal life, she had been a lady, and one in love, until the day it was all over. She and Antonio still wear the clothes in which they were put in their caskets. Antonio still wears his suit with the handkerchief in its breast pocket, and never takes off his bowtie. They talk all the time about getting new clothes, because they're not "truly dead," but their hunger always makes them forget.

Antonio holds Anika against the floor and kisses her breasts. Blood gives them life. Her fangs come out with thirst and heat and she bites his neck. Antonio also drinks from her, then they share each other's bloods with a kiss. Their wounds close eventually with the blood they have consumed from others, which gives them a strange vitality.

They hear the thunder and the rain. When they are done, they kiss one another a long time. Then they get up.

"I'm suddenly hungry again," Anika says. "The night is still young. The dawn far away."

"Let us go," Antonio says. "We should get new clothes, too."

"Shall we get a drink this time? Alcohol hasn't lost its grip."

"Yes, I would like that, so that I can taste it from your breath."

They go out again.

3

Joanna Riddler steps out of the taxi on Cloud Ave. and Thunder St. and walks one block to a large house in the corner. Lately, she's been coming home late, and her husband already suspects something. He is a quiet man and doesn't readily confront her, but he knows something's up.

"Have you taken your medicine?" she asks after greeting him and kissing him on the cheek. He's by the fire, reading the newspaper.

"Doctor couldn't tell what was the matter with me and told me to stop taking it, just in case that's what's making me sick."

"Well, as a nurse, I must contradict him. That medicine can only make you better. Shall I bring it to you?"

"I'm glad you're concerned," Mr. Riddler says. "But…I think I want to lay it off for a while."

"Ok, can I pour you a drink?" she asks.

"That sounds like a lovely idea," he says.

Joanna gets a bottle of cognac from one of the shelves and pours it in a glass with ice. She stirs it vigorously for a while with a spoon. When she's done, she washes the spoon thoroughly with soap and places it in a solution to disinfect it. She hands the drink to her husband.

"Quite strong," he says as she watches him drink it.

"It's cognac, my dear," she answers. "Come, drink up. It will help you go to sleep. Lately, you've been having bad nights."

He looks at the drink a moment, and then downs it.

"Thank you," he says, and continues reading the paper.

"You're such a good boy," Joanna says and goes up to the bedroom.

At night, Mr. Riddler is pale. He complains of some pain, and says he should go to the hospital.

The phone in the bedroom, Joanna says, is not working, "for some reason." She goes downstairs even as her husband tells her to help him to the car, so that she can drive him to the emergency room. She waits a few moments before calling for an ambulance.

When she returns to the bedroom, her husband is up on his feet and shivering. Despite his mix of black and white, he's become completely a white man, so pale he is. Joanna helps him downstairs, but tells him that the ambulance is coming, and that they should wait for it.

It takes the ambulance about ten minutes to arrive, by which time Mr. Riddler has fallen unconscious. The paramedics lay him on the stretcher and take him to the hospital.

Joanna sits with him and holds his hand in the hospital room before the nurses. When the nurses are gone, Mr. Riddler wakes up. He is thirsty. There is a jar of water in the room. Joanna takes a little cup, pours the water, and stirs it. She gives it to her husband. After drinking the water, he is sick again.

Joanna waits a little before calling the nurses. When the nurses arrive, they call for the doctor. When the doctor arrives, he doesn't know what to do. The charts show nothing that could be the matter with him. It is a strange disease.

That night, Mr. Riddler dies.

Joanna wants to have him cremated, but Mr. Riddler's lawyers produce papers where Mr. Riddler *specifically* stated he wanted to be buried. Joanna is angry and threatens a lawsuit against the lawyers.

Two months later, Joanna receives a million dollars in insurance money, keeps the house, and a large part of Mr. Riddler's fortune.

Mr. Riddler is buried in an open cemetery among beautiful green grass. Yet not everyone is happy that the case of his death is closed. Three months after Mrs. Riddler receives Mr. Riddler's fortune, Mr. Riddler's sons from his first marriage want the forensic examiners to conduct a forensic test. They suspect their father was poisoned. After some legal battles, it is decided that Mr. Riddler's body will be exhumed.

Some days after the order, Mr. Riddler's grave is found open and empty. Joanna and her lover, fearing to lose everything, dug him out, put him in the covered back of a pickup truck, and took him to an old, abandoned cemetery, where no one would think to look for him. No body. No crime.

They found a way into the tomb where stone coffins are above ground, pickaxed the floor, dug out a grave, and put Mr. Riddler in it. Because his body was well-embalmed, he still looked in good shape. Once his body was in the hole, they put the dirt back on top of him and left the chamber, just as dawn was approaching.

Joanna was suspected for a long time of digging out the body, but survived the criminal ordeal and charges that followed. She still lives in the opulent house, though her lover moved on. A year later, he committed suicide.

Now lying in his hole, without the earth back on him, Arthur Riddler thinks of the times he was ill. He knows his wife killed him because he saw her pour the solution in his cup of water at the hospital. Every time she gave him something to drink, he got sick.

Arthur Riddler still thinks of those days.

"Oh, but I loved you! How could you?" he says. He's sitting in his grave. He's in pain. "Why was my life so important that you should do that? Wasn't there another alternative? How about a richer man? It would have broken my heart, but I would have been able to move on. To start again. But I must rest. In my stage of life, I need rest. The dead need rest. Rest from memories."

He turns in the hole like it is a mattress, and closes his eyes.

4

❝So you're a vampire," Anika asks Albert, who goes by the Italianized name of *Albertini*. He and his girlfriend, Antonietta, are on their way to a posh "vampire club" in Livelife called "Bloodwine."

Anika and Antonio are in the town of Magnolias. The sidewalks are full of young people going to and from bars. Some sit at open cafes, others on the sidewalks, and smoke cigarettes.

Upon their arrival, they asked people about the best store to get clothes. Albertini stopped to answer, "They are closed at this time. But those are elegant clothes, you should drop by Bloodwine. You cut the part. Are you vampires? Antonietta and I go by that label."

That led to Anika to ask him if he was, in fact, a vampire.

Albertini's reply was quick, and it came with a gallant nod. "Yes."

On him is a black Dracula's cape, and in his mouth a pair of canines sharpened to points. His girlfriend, long-haired and blond, is in a tight-fitting black dress, the top of which is intentionally diaphanous. She's not wearing a bra, and has on her black shoes with thick, high heels.

"Oh, it is truly lovely to meet you," Anika says. "It is hard to meet people like yourself nowadays."

"We are a rare breed, indeed," Albertini admits.

"We too are a couple," Anika says of her and Antonio. "Dead for many years. We only come out once a week, or when we are hungry.

Though today we want to drink as well."

"Oh, then you should really stop by Bloodwine," Albertini says.

"Oh, it is really so nice to meet you!" Antonietta says, suddenly. She has been staring at Anika and Antonio with lust and admiration. "You are so lovely."

Anika curtsies.

"You got that down pat," Albertini says, impressed.

"Oh God, that was so hot," Antonietta says. "I've never seen anyone do it so well. I have to learn."

"Thank you," Anika answers. "Old habits are hard to break. How often do you go out for blood?"

Albertini laughs. "Oh, not that often. We only drink of each other now and then." He points to Antonietta. "Unless we have company that shares our love for that beautiful nectar."

Anika is surprised. "You have other vampire friends? Are you in a clan?"

Albertini laughs again. "You could say that! They are all at Bloodwine."

"And you all share blood with one another?"

"Yes, if they are the right people, we do."

"That is very interesting," Anika says. "Ever since my first night as someone...different...I've only had the blood of one vampire, the love of my life—or my death—Antonio."

Antonio bows. Albertini and Antonietta look at each other. Albertini looks at his girlfriend with raised eyebrows. Antonietta nods her head emphatically and smiles. Then she looks at Antonio and Anika, biting her lips.

"You should indeed meet us at Bloodwine," Albertini says.

"Sounds like an appetizing place," Anika replies. "Lately, our social life has been quite...dead."

"One question," Antonietta says. "Are you a good kisser?"

"Me?" Anika asks. "I will let Antonio be the judge."

"When she kisses me, I feel like I live again," Antonio says.

"That is so romantic," Antonietta says. She looks at Anika with desire. "What about a test? I can tell you if you're a good kisser."

Anika looks at Antonio.

"Interesting vampires," she says. "Yes, tell me. Will you use your tongue?"

"Oh, no problem," Antonietta says.

Antonio moves to the side. The girls kiss.

There is cheer from many young men on the sidewalk. When they are finished kissing, Anika says,

"I can sense much blood, much life, in you," she says. "You are well fed or are a unique vampire. Will you share some of that with me?"

"Oh, after that, I will share my world with you," Antonietta answers.

Anika smiles. "So I suppose it was good."

"It was beautiful."

Albertini smiles at Antonio, holds Antonietta by the waist, and repeats his invitation regarding Bloodwine.

"Maybe we can go with you," Anika says. "Will you fly?"

"No, we rather walk," Albertini says, laughing. "We like to live like humans."

The four walk to Bloodwine.

When they get to the club, they are required to pay to get in.

"Pay!" Anika exclaims. "At a vampire club?"

Antonietta is too lusty for Anika and Antonio, and convinces Albertini to pay for them. Once the tickets have been bought, they present them at the door. The bouncers put a tag on Anika and Antonio's wrists. The lovers look at them with interest, as if they had gotten watches. They go in.

They are greeted by loud, electric, industrial sounds. Laser lights spear across the large dance floor and cross one another like glowing javelins.

"What horrendous music!" Anika exclaims. There are many people wearing black and red leather. The motion of their bodies and arms to the music catches Anika's attention. It's like a strange form of meditative dance, not in sync with the harsh and quick moving sounds.

"It's just starting," Albertini says. "It gets better afterwards."

"I will buy you a drink," Antonietta says to Anika. "What will you have?"

"What do you recommend?" Anika asks.

"How about a Bloody Margarita?"

"Oh, yes, that sounds delicious," Anika responds.

"And you, my fellow, what will you have?" Albertini asks Antonio.

"Anything you're having will be an excellent choice," Antonio replies.

After getting the drinks, they go into a dim room full of couches. Cigarette and weed smoke are prevalent. A woman with long canines is tied to the wall in one part of the room. She is completely naked. A man in a black mask whips on her nipples, her legs, and her arms. Nearby, a man shines a small flashlight into the yellow eyes of another man.

Albertini and Antonietta seem to know them all.

"We found these two vampires lost in Magnolias," Albertini says to a group sitting near them.

Many have sharp canines, though many look fake.

"You are a vampire, too?" Antonio asks a man he just met.

"I am," the man says, sighing as if that is one of the truths of life that can't be avoided. "Pleasure to meet you. I am Robert." He shakes Antonio's hand. "The night is cold," he says, for Antonio's hand is cold.

Anika is confused. They all call themselves vampires, but feel warm in the flesh. There is a lot perspiration on their skins. She feels she ought to get out more, for these vampires surely hadn't lost the smell of raw, human flesh. The woman getting her nipples whipped intrigues her, however. Anika pinches herself through the top of her dress as if to recreate a similar sensation. Antonietta interrupts her thoughts and invites her to dance.

Anika is shocked. "Dance? To this music? I remember the days of ragtime and the Hesitation Waltz. Did you ever dance it?"

"Waltz? No, but that would be lovely to learn, if you could teach it to me," Antonietta says.

"Perhaps I will, if I ever remember the steps."

"Come, let's go dance," Albertini says, taking Antonietta's hand. He feels that Anika is not the dancing type.

Other people offer and get Anika a drink. Half an hour later, Antonietta and Albertini return, looking a little tipsy. There is a little more conversation. After some time, Antonietta takes off one of her shoes and stretches her leg toward Anika. Anika stares down as Antonietta's foot makes its way under her dress.

Antonietta is dreamy. "Will you teach me how to waltz now?" she asks.

"Where?" Anika replies, lifting her gaze.

"I'll show you." She turns to whisper to Albertini.

Albertini consents to what Antonietta tells him.

Antonietta turns to Anika.

"Let us get out of here," she says.

When they're outside, Albertini says,

"Instead of flying, we'll take a cab." He laughs.

The taxi takes them to a small house outside main Magnolias, where Antonietta pulls down the top of her black dress and invites Anika to suck. Anika looks at Antonietta with surprise, but obliges. Antonietta sighs and holds Anika's head.

But Anika is still hungry for blood, and Albertini and Antonietta promised to give them some.

"Are you ready to share you world with me?" she says to Antonietta after a moment.

"Oh, God, that is so hot!" Antonietta says. She offers her neck.

"Just like that?" Anika asks.

"Yes," Antonietta says, sighing with desire. "Why are you making me wait?"

Antonietta expects tender lovemaking to her neck. When she feels Anika's fangs tear into her skin, she immediately panicks.

"There it is," Antonio says, pointing at the two girls, smiling, sitting next to Albertini. Albertini admires the scene a moment, then his smile goes away, noticing a strange thing: Antonietta's struggle to free herself from Anika.

"Ok, that should be it," he says. "I think you're biting too hard."

"You think?" Antonio asks.

"Yeah, looks like it."

Albertini sits back and crosses his arms, confused. Then his concern makes him get up. Anika won't let go of Antonietta, and as she drinks, she becomes more ravenous.

"Ok, that's enough!" Albertini says out loud.

But Anika won't let go.

Albertini begins to move forward. "Hey, I said stop!"

Antonio blocks him with his arm. "You promised her blood!" In a moment, he looks larger, bestial. His eyes are flashing red. His fangs are truer in form than Albertini's little canines.

The suddenness of this transformation sends a shudder down Albertini's spine

He retreats, exclaiming. "What the fuck! Get out of my house!" A part of him tells him the eyes and the fangs are a trick. Still, he hadn't seen them before. Confused and terrified, he backs further away.

"Why promise blood and give us nothing!" Antonio's voice is rough and strong. All of a sudden, he makes a motion to get up.

"Get the fuck out!" Albertini yells, backing away even more. Suddenly, he turns and runs into a room. He reappears, quickly, holding a gun.

"Stop, you bitch! Or I'll shoot!"

As he sees Antonio approach, he lets out a bullet. The bullet only grazes Antonio's jacket.

Antonio's flight is almost as quick as the bullet. In no time, Albertini is toppled to the floor as if by a two-ton building.

Antonio devours him, drains him.

"Oh, she's human! No vampire after all," Anika says, wiping the blood off her mouth and licking her hand.

"It was so after all," Antonio says. "I suspected it."

Anika looks toward Antonietta's unconscious body on the floor.

"What are you thinking?" Antonio asks.

"I have a thought," Anika says. "We haven't had company in a while."

"That is true," Antonio says.

"So, what do you think of...?" She points at Antonietta. "She would be a great consort. Yes, for both of us. We'd have a new companion."

"Lovely idea, though the caskets are a little small at the waist."

"She's a small thing," Anika replies. "My bed has room. It was evidently destined for someone else before I poked my head in. Oh, lucky death! She'll fit in with me on one side."

"That is true, and you have a pillow. It will still be a little tight."

"Better to share our warmth. At least after we're fed."

Antonio nods, then looks toward Albertini. "What about him? I think I drank too much from him. I would not like adverse allegiances."

"Neither would I. Break his neck. Better yet, bury a stake in his heart, so that he won't follow us."

But Antonio doesn't have a stake, and he can't see one anywhere. The only weapons around are knives and Albertini's gun, but they don't kill vampires. Unable to know what to do, Antonio digs his suddenly-enlarged nails into Albertini's flesh, breaks a rib, and removes the heart from his body. Then he cuts off Albertini's head with a knife.

"Enjoy your death!" he says toward Albertini, then looks at Anika, who is observing him. "When he comes back to life, if he does, he'll have no head."

Anika nods, then looks around.

"What is it?" Antonio asks.

"There is someone here." Anika points. "It comes from that door." She walks to it, listens, and then opens it. A cat flies out at great speed and shoots down the hall. Anika backs out more surprised than frightened, then looks into the room. Very soon, she is enthralled. Before her is a closet bursting at the seams. Antonio comes to her side. "Look at all that," she says. "Clothes!"

They look at each other and go in. Anika finds many dresses she likes. Albertini is a little on the small side, but there are jackets and shoes that fit Antonio, perfectly.

"Oh, she likes red and black," Anika says, inspecting Antonietta's dresses. She pulls out a black overcoat and holds it against her. "Oh, she won't mind to share."

"From now on, we'll share everything," Antonio says.

Anika dons the overcoat and Antonio a jacket and a red tie. They put the rest of the clothes in a suitcase, along with perfumes, candles and other items they find in the house. Antonio picks up Antonietta.

They are back in the crypt around two-thirty. Antonio deposits Antonietta in Anika's casket. The way he does is tender, laying her softly on the pillow inside, like she was a new treasure.

"I wonder when she'll wake up?" Anika asks.

"It might be soon, a few hours or a few days," Antonio says. "She will be starving. Which means we must go out, so that she can feed. She'll want more than just our blood."

Anika looks toward the zombie's grave. "Wait! We haven't put the dirt back on Engusanado."

"True," Antonio says. "Let's do it."

Together, they cover Engusanado with the earth he displaces every time he comes out. They do it with the shovels left there during his internment. When their mission is accomplished, they put the shovels behind one of the caskets and take each other. They make love on the crypt's floor. The blood they have consumed makes their body more sensitive and puts them in a romantic trance. Once the silver glow appears at the top of the open trapdoor, they are ready to sleep. Antonio lifts the lid for Anika to get in. Anika lies down next to Antonietta.

"From now on," Antonio says, kissing Anika's hand; "I must serve two."

He puts the lid down over Anika and Antonietta and goes to his own "bed" to sleep.

5

At nine the next night, Anika, Antonio and Antonietta are still asleep. Engusanado stirs from his death's slumber and breaks out of the dirt above him. He has been dreaming of Joanna.

"How can the dead dream?" he says. "It is a restless death." He rubs his forehead with his somewhat bony hand. "I don't think I'll be at peace while I think of you, my love," he says. "I wonder where you are now. You said if I ever died, you'd keep the place, because you liked it that it was so close to the little lake with all the boats."

He looks up then turns his head right. Against the bier of Anika's casket is a suitcase. Edges of clothes stick out because it is filled to the brim.

Engusanado gets up slowly and walks to it, slowly, limping like all zombies do. He examines the suitcase, toys with the clasps and pulls up the long, retrievable handle on top. He's attempting to get in. After a long while of constant failure, he pushes one of the buttons—just to see what happens. The clasps spring up. Engusanado himself springs a little, as if the clasps had become alive. Despite the little scare, he is not dissuaded. Their jumping might mean something. He has the right thinking. He pulls up the clasps and then the top of the suitcase like he was prying open a mouth. He is happy. As he stares at all the clothes, a thought springs up. He raises up his bright eyes in contemplation of an idea, then looks back down. There is so much clothes in the suitcase. It is a closet shrunk to a small size. Dresses, pants, shirts, ties, and long capes appear. There are also candles and matches.

Engusanado rubs a bony finger on his bony chin. He doesn't think Antonio and Anika would mind if he borrowed a few items. They are good people. Good vampires. Good to him. He finds Antonio's old suit jacket and a pair of pants. On top of it all, he dons the cape. Despite his eyes that serve as lamps in the darkness, they don't afford a very colorful visual. He picks up a candle and a box of matches. After almost five minutes of striking several matches, he manages to make a flame and light the wick. He takes the candle to his grave. Now with the light, he looks down at what is wearing. He is excited, almost as if he was looking in the mirror.

"Look at you, ol' zombie!" he says. "You look all dandy!"

He exits the crypt, leaving the suitcase closed but unclasped.

He doesn't know what he's doing, but he's suddenly out on the road.

Sunday nights are dead nights in Magnolias and there are very few people around. Those who are see an old, slow, slouching man on the sidewalk. Most ignore him, though they close their noses because the air suddenly stinks of death. A few catch a glimpse of his face under the cape's hood and widen their eyes before retreating at great speed. Others look back at him and wonder if he has some disease. His swarthy face is swollen in places, and his eyeballs are large. A young man asks him if he needs some help.

"No," Engusanado says, without pausing or looking at him. The young man closes his nose with his fingers and dashes away, quickly. Engusanado keeps walking. Suddenly, he has a destination.

Many things have changed in the world he once inhabited, but Engusanado recognizes a few old things in his murky memory.

He reaches the old neighborhood at last. This he remembers. So little has changed. It has been so long since he last saw it, he feels as if he is just returning from some little trip and is finally getting back home. His house is still in the corner. The little lake and the boats are behind it a mile away down Lake St., on the other side of the backyard's wall.

He goes slowly up the inclined steps to what once was his front door. When he reaches the door, he stares at it a long time. There are so many memories on it. It is the same door. He can see it clearly within the shadows of the night like a still memory. His mental vision goes past it to the boats on the lake, their sails, and the water. Then he looks down the steps. He remembers the days he used to walk down to his car to go to work, his briefcase in hand, the joy he felt at returning to his love, to his Joanna!

A storm of memories stirs all the leaves in his brain. He remembers his wedding day, full of light, when he brought young Joanna up to the door, up the inclined steps in his arms, her hair moving lightly in the wind, her smile and soft laughter.

He rests a hand and his head on the door. He suddenly hears the music of the old piano, as if the keys were being played in his ears. Joanna used to love *Silence* by Beethoven. She used to play it often, as if she was always sad, though she was always smiling at the end of it.

A lone car passes by. The driver does not see him and Engusanado is too wrapped in his memories to pay any attention to it.

"Oh, Joanna, love of my life," he says. "Why did you turn so dark? It might scare you to see little old me now after so long gone. Gone from your memory, perhaps. But I won't live—or be dead—in peace unless I know why. Perhaps you're lonely, lonely inside your heart though not in company? Have no compassion for me if you have changed. Being dead is not so bad, though the memories kill you sometimes. The good memories. But sometimes the bad ones, too. Maybe…maybe if I fixed the bad memories with fresh, good ones? Memories that have not gone through the ravage of long longing but are so near you could almost touch them? Like lips that come back to lips just to touch again the kiss they have in their memory?

"Oh! Forgive the words of the dead! We think in dead ways. I would love to show you my new place. It is a lonely chamber, but I have two good friends who put the earth back on me so that I may sleep my dead-man's sleep. You might say that me standing here reeks of revenge. No, no, my love. But if it *is* revenge, it is bound with love. Oh, dear Joanna, love and revenge *can* be friends, indeed. We've had a long spat, you and I. But isn't marriage a fight? After the fight comes the peace and a stronger union, the touch of immortal hands bound together in immortal love, such as Antonio and Anika have, who look after each other, and even look after me."

He pauses a moment, and thinks that he may have made a mistake.

"Perhaps you don't live here anymore. But that can't be so. Whatever leads the dead tells me you're still here, and the dead is never wrong.

You are still here. I also know you are alone. Living alone cannot be happiness. Maybe if you tried to be dead a little? The dead also have adventures. Have you ever tasted living worms? They live in the soil. They wriggle in your mouth somewhat, and when you bite them, you can sense the juice that comes out of them. I think they're delicious. That is adventurous, aye?"

Engusanado puts his hand on the cold doorknob. He tries to turn it, but it won't give. It is locked. He remembers, however, that he used to leave the key under the mat outside the door. He bends to look for it, but finds nothing. How to get in? He goes into a deep concentration and suddenly he's on the other side.

He did not know he had this power, but suddenly looks around. It is all dark inside. Even his dead eyes can only see shadows. The staircase is dark as well, perhaps from some broken light. With his slow, dead, almost disabled step, Engusanado goes up.

Joanna is beginning to doze off. She likes sleeping with the lights off. Suddenly, she hears light steps on the staircase. She pauses from adjusting her pillow and listens. She decides it is her imagination when the steps stop and lays her head down again. She is fifty-five years old now, three times married after Arthur and three times divorced.

Arthur's company went bankrupt after his passing, the company that he built and that he had worked on for ten years, which gave him the money that she took from him in a lazy way, the laziest way possible—murder.

She is an unhappy woman, never satisfied, and has forgotten all her crimes as if they never happened. Her life has been one of lawsuits against people for their money. One day, she claimed that a restaurant had poisoned her with expired meat. She sued the owner successfully for fifty-thousand dollars. Another time, she claimed the coffee in her cup was too hot. She sued the coffee shop for a million dollars and won.

Arthur's fortune was not so large in her esteem, only about five million dollars—yet it was five million dollars that he had put sweat and blood into making—which she decided to take, anyway. But she didn't take the money from him alone, but from his children.

She doesn't hear him when he arrives.

Engusanado just stands there, watching her. He doesn't know how to start. "Joanna?" "Hello dear?" "Good Evening?"

"Do you still play that beautiful music in the piano?" he asks.

Up Joanna jumps. She sees the shadow of Engusanado and screams.

"Get out! Who are you?" She makes a dash for the bedside lamp to turn it on, to make sure she is not seeing things. Engusanado replies,

"Arthur, your husband."

The lamp is knocked to the floor. Joanna slaps the bed, frantically, screaming, "No! No! No! No! No! No!" shaking her head with her eyes closed. Then she freezes, begins to cry. She loses her voice. She is suddenly unable to even move a finger. Engusanado begins to walk to her.

"Why did you kill me?" he asks.

Joanna pees on herself and the bed. Then her heart begins to fail. She drops back, unconscious. Engusanado gets to her.

"Joanna?" he asks.

But Joanna can't even hear the dead. Engusanado touches her face.

"Still beautiful," he says; "though older. Old is beautiful."

He puts his face close to hers.

"Do you remember me, love?" he asks. "Perhaps you have remembered me. You had forgotten me. I'm sorry for coming to you this way, but there was no other way. Does the dead have any other way? Oh, so beautiful. I could kiss you."

He leans over her and kisses her with his worm- and death-infected breath. Then he looks at her again.

"You killed me, you bitch!" he cries. "Revenge through love? No, love through revenge. Or it is the same thing? Come with me, my love."

He lays his ear on her chest.

"A little beat," he says. "That cannot be." He puts his bony hands around her throat and strangles her until her life goes out of her. Then he puts her on his back. It is a long way to toil, but the night is old and Magnolias is asleep. Not a pair of legs about, no one out for a cigarette. A police car passes by. Engusanado says,

"We're almost there, my love. You'll meet new friends."

He's at his grave at three in the morning. He puts Joanna in his hole, the one that she herself had dug.

"Tomorrow, I'll make a bigger hole where we both fit in," he says.

He throws the dirt on her. If strangulation didn't kill her, lack of oxygen will. Engusanado lies down and turns to the mound of earth covering her. He caresses the earth.

"My love has returned," he says, and closes his eyes.

6

At five-thirty in the morning, Antonietta screams. It is a scream of terror. It is the awakening of the dead when its death was violent. The sound is a knife in the dark quiet of the crypt. It is so piercing, it is a surprise the zombie outside doesn't wake up. But she rouses Anika, who is sleeping next to her.

Anika hears her pawing the lid of the coffin.

"Be quiet, love," she says. "Everything will be fine from now on. You are among friends, eternal friends who will be your support till the end of time."

Antonietta hears and feels the presence. Their bodies are touching each other.

"Who are you? Where am I?" Antonietta asks, in panicked confusion.

"You are home. And I am Anika, your best friend in the world."

"Anika!" Antonietta exclaims. "Who are you? What are you doing here? Or what am I doing here? Where am I?"

"That's the same question twice," Anika replies. "I told you, you are home."

"My…my home?"

"Yes, for eternity. But maybe I understand why you woke up. You are hungry. Is that what it is?"

"I am…thirsty," Antonietta says.

"It is the same thing to us. Unless…" Anika pauses a moment, suspiciously; "it is water you want?"

"No, not water. I want…I don't know what I want."

"I know what you want," Anika says. "Come closer to me. Move your body over mine. There is room enough to raise yourself a little. I'll lead you." She puts her hand behind Antonietta's head and leads her to her. "Go ahead. I won't scream. I will like the pain."

Antonietta smells Anika's throat. Smells blood. This means her transformation is complete. Her fangs come out by themselves. They pierce into Anika's neck by instinct.

Anika gasps a little and closes her eyes. The bite is arousing. She strokes the back of Antonietta's head. She feels a soft, climatic sensation.

"Oh, yes, just like that," she says, lost in the moment.

"Oh, I feel much better!" Antonietta says. "That was what I needed. Oh, I can rest now! I will rest now."

"Yes, we'll have to get out sooner than I thought," Anika says. "You took much from me. But now, we are bound. We share something. Now sleep. If you rise before I do and wish to get out, push the lid—this" (she leads Antonietta's hand to it) "and it will open. You are strong enough, now. But I suggest you sleep. It might not be good wandering around now."

"I will sleep, now," Antonietta says. But she can't close her eyes. She looks around the darkness a long while, and when Anika is asleep—she sleeps deeply like the dead at this time of the morning—she pushes up the 400 lbs lid with ease and sits up. It is still dark outside, except for a grey light coming in through the open trapdoor and a cool breeze.

She rises from the coffin and gets on the floor. She notices Engusanado. He doesn't move, doesn't breathe, yet something tells her he is another one that wakes up from time to time.

Antonietta follows the grey light up the steps and exits the trapdoor. She knows she is somone because she is moving. She's got animation. Yet if you asked her who she is, she wouldn't know.

She is outside the trapdoor. She sees the window and the closed door. She nears the window, lays her hands on the sill, and looks outside.

The world is a dark grey curtain of stars. Her eyes are slightly red from long sleep and from drinking blood. The marks of the fangs that caused her death are now closed on her neck, and dry lines of the blood she drank from Anika run from her lips.

Antonietta's eyes wander into the garden. The red rose, clothed in darkness, wavering lightly, catches her attention like a painting catches a passersby's attention. Her new vision makes the obscured color jump out a little. She sees the trace of red within the meager light. Yet as the night dress begins to dissipate, and the edges of things in the garden begin to clear, the rose becomes a sort of clock. Parts of it begin to brighten, to fade back into color and to turn vivid. Sunlight is a slow walker behind the graves and trees. Then the first beam clears an angel of stone. The ray of dawn strikes the window.

It's a sudden bite. Antonietta crosses her arms over her face and screams. She immediately casts herself to the floor and crawls at lightning speed to the other side of the room. Once in the safety of the corner's shadows, she looks at the back of her arms. She can tell they are burned by the different shade of color from the rest of her skin. Her face has suffered a little as well, but it has only turned red, though she can't see it. Her cheeks hurt. But the burn in her arms is enough to give her alarm. That tells her that ray of sun is an enemy!

She is lost in a limbo of memory. She realizes it now as she sits on her heels and covers her face with her hands. She senses that a page of her life turned before she got to the end of it.

And she is angry at the sun for giving her the night as her only friend. She will only look at the sea when it is dark.

She goes with sadness down the steps again. She doesn't recall many things, though there are things she ought to know that she doesn't know. It's like a moment when one has to remember things yet one is unable to.

Once back in the crypt, Antonietta looks around. She knows something is out of place, yet doesn't know what. One thing she knows, she is trapped. Outside the trapdoor, there is death. Here, a life in darkness.

When she reaches Anika's casket, she sits on her heels again and cries. She cries whatever tears remain over a past that wants to be her present. She's aware she has lost her memory, and that is the biggest pain and her greatest terror. Not to know who you are is the greatest terror of all.

She lies down, facing the place where she now sleeps, and lays her right arm over her face, over her eyes, as if to block the eternal darkness that is now her world. There she now sleeps.

When the clock of the world strikes eight that evengin, Antonio rises. He sees Antonietta on the floor. On the other side, he sees Engusanado, who is outside his grave, and wearing his clothes. His hand is on the dirt that fills the grave. Antonio wonders why the hole is filled with the earth and Engusanado not under it.

He doesn't think long. He looks back at the figure of Antonietta. He approaches her, sits on his heels behind her, and leans over to kiss and lick her neck.

Antonietta doesn't quite awake, but feels, in her dreamy state, lips kissing her. She raises her arm off her face and wraps it around the kisser.

"Antonio and Antonietta," Antonio whispers. "The gods of the night have brought us together."

Antonietta accepts his kiss in her mouth, on her breasts, on her throat.

"My name is Antonio?" she asks.

Antonio strokes her hair. He has seen her state before. "No, you are the Antonietta, the one of my dreams, the one who completes my name."

When Anika wakes up, she smells the scent of the raw intimacy between Antonio and Antonietta. She sits up and watches them. Antonietta is dreamy. Her long black dress has ridden up to the top of her thighs and Antonio is on top of her. Anika contemplates them and strokes her throat with her hand. Antonietta drinks from Antonio's throat as Antonio raises and lowers himself onto her, making her delirious.

Antonio grunts and falls over Antonietta.

"Now you are mine!" he says.

"So I see," Anika says.

"And she's yours too, my love," he replies. He lifts himself with his arms and looks down at Antonietta. Antonietta looks back with red-shot blue eyes. "We're hers, too." Antonio strokes her cheek, tenderly, "Did you see the garden, my love?"

Antonietta doesn't answer. She smiles and turns her face. She looks toward the open trapdoor steps that normal eyes would not see. She can see the room and the steps as if a gray light had been turned on. Her sight comes from the light of her eyes, the torch of the vampires.

She turns back to look at Antonio. The blood she drank from him is on her chin and running to her throat. Like a cat licks its young, Antonio licks it off.

"Come, now, our lover," he says, getting up.

Antonietta sits up. Antonio helps her up.

"We shall explore the night," he says. He stretches his hand to Anika, who is still sitting in her casket. "You too, my love."

Anika holds his hand and gets out. Antonio, in the center, holds both their hands as they go up the steps. The moon is on the window, full and bright. It greets their eyes. The three lean their pale, almost sheeny white hands on the windowsill. It is almost as if the moon penetrates their skin and gives them a glow, the way it does a thriafae. It mesmerizes and traps with its beauty, though Anika and Antonio like the chase more than romantic entrapments.

Antonietta marks the moon like it is a new discovery. It seems like an angel floating in the sky. It seems close, almost as if she could touch it. Her hand goes to the window. She is still in a dreamy state. After a moment, she turns to her companions. She looks at their faces as they stare into the world.

Whatever emotion she now has, it has bowed to the inevitable. She does not yet care deeply for these strangers that she lusted over in her human life, yet where would she go? She doesn't even know who she is, or what feelings she had for them. She no longer knows the world. She would dread stepping into it alone, without society, without beings who share her essence. Outside the loss of memory, being alone is the dead's greatest fear. All the same, reality sinks in. She is someone, she feels, that she ought to be. She craves blood.

She leans closer to the window. She has no breath to dampen the pane.

"Now, where shall we go?" Antonio says. "Night gives a road. No rain will dampen the will of the evening jogger, the lonely walker." He looks at Antonietta. "It is time to use your wings. We will share everything."

This reassures Antonietta. She will not be hungry, and she will not be alone. Still, she closes her eyes. She knows something has changed. She felt it with the sun. She wasn't who she *was* at that moment. Some past cried in her, tried to call her back, call back what was dead. Something seems gone. Something feels missed. She ought to have loved the sun. She remembers it. She looks at Antonio.

"Ok," she says and looks down.

After having drunk from Antonio and Anika, she's not very hungry, but feels she must accompany them. She doesn't know why, yet neither how she could be without them.

Antonio holds both their hands as they fly to Magnolias. Antonietta doesn't let go, as if afraid she might lose them. Far beneath her, the moving heads of people walking the street seem like the heads of cattle, and Antonietta can smell their blood. Without her knowing, her whole being has been altered. She feels the strangeness of this, even if she can't pinpoint the source or its beginning, or any prior knowledge that she ever saw them differently.

They descend far from view, though Magnolias is mostly empty. It is around eleven and a Monday. There aren't many people around. Only some stores are open, and here and there a café. The emptiness of the city works to Antonio and Anika's advantage every time they visit, it affords more secrecy.

Always, before a hunt, they scout the terrain seeking the weakest prey, the lost lamb, the way a lion would scout a herd of buffaloes. Unlike the lion that looks from afar, however, they like to come amongst the herd for a closer inspection. Old folks they dismiss, or people who don't appear to be healthy.

Here and there, people walk out of the cafés, but few go farther than a car parked on the street. Three young people, two men and a woman, all in their young twenties, walk out of a store carrying bags of chips and soda bottles. Antonietta stares at their throats.

"Hey, Antonietta!" one of the men says.

Antonietta! Oh yes, that's the name Antonio gave her, she remembers. Antonietta looks mystified at the man who seems to know it. The fog in her window, however, seems to lift a bit. She feels has seen him and his two companions before.

"Hey, it's me, Robert!" says the man, as if he can tell Antonietta's confusion. Then he looks at Antonio and Anika. "Hey, we met on Saturday!" He stretches his hand.

Antonio frowns a little and then recognizes him. "Oh, yes!" he bows and smiles as he takes the hand. "What a coincidence."

"What a classy bow," says the girl in Robert's company. Her name is Justine and she has pretty brown eyes.

"Wow," Robert says. "Six vampires together! Why are you all guys dressed up? Not done partying?" He looks at Antonietta. "Why are you still wearing the same dress from Saturday?"

Antonietta frowns now. Such a comment about her dress offends any woman, dead or alive.

"You say you are a vampire?" she asks, suddenly.

Robert is taken aback, as if offended. "What kind of question is that?

We all are! What a question! Don't you recognize us? Where is Albertini?"

"He went early to his grave," Antonio says.

Robert and his companions laugh and clap. "Early to his grave!"

Justine catches Antonietta's serious glance. "You're acting strange, Antonietta," she says.

Antonietta is serious, and looks at Justine with an inquistive glance. "Are you a vampire?" she asks Justine.

Robert is even more taken aback. "Are you on drugs?" he says. "What is the matter with you?"

"Do you have blood to share?" Anika asks.

Robert raises his eyebrows. "Blood to share!"

"Yes," Anika answers. "We'd like some. Forgive Antonietta. She is thirsty. And all of us being vampires, we thought you might have blood to share."

"As a matter of fact, I do," says Justine. "It's in the freezer. Chilled, you know? Or it could be frozen by now."

"That's not good anymore," says Robert. "Thawing it is bad."

"We'll take anything," Anika says.

"Why would you want frozen blood?" Justine asks.

"We don't mind that," Antonio says. "How much do you have of that?"

Justine puts her index and thumb half an inch apart. "About this much."

"Yeah, but we're not doing that right now," Robert says.

Anika pulls down the top of her dress, though not all the way. She is still a lady, though also hungry.

"I will let you suck here," she says. The top of her areolas are visible.

Robert is the type of man who has said no many times to a woman's temptation, but every day is not the same day. He knows too much about the young, fake vampire culture to know where such gestures lead. He has done far less for drugs. What is a little bit of frozen blood that can end his night in a better way? Both Anika and Antonietta are beautiful, for he has included Antonietta in anything that might follow.

"Can I suck there, too?" Justine asks.

"Of course," Anika says.

"By the way, my name is Justine."

"It's a pleasure, Justine!"

In the minds of the young men, this meeting has evolved into an orgy in waiting, and are very unwilling to let it pass by. One could, but he knows that the other would go along with it, thus both men say yes.

"By the way," Antonio asks, smiling as they walk to Robert's house. "Do you have any stakes?"

Robert laughs. "Steaks? Like pieces of meat?"

"Wooden stakes," Antonio says.

"Yes, we won't be using them. You only use that on real vampires. I have them just in case they pop up, you know." He laughs at the end of this sentence. "Why do you want to know?"

"Oh, I'd like to buy some for my collection, in case real vampires pop up."

"Oh, I see. Yes, I have many."

The other young man introduces himself as Enrique. He's the youngest of the three, only twenty-two, but also the tallest. He looks at Anika with love and lust. Anika pays him the compliment of a smile.

Robert's house is in a street with barely any lights. He has a collection of stakes in black holsters upon the livingroom's wall. There are many CD's in shelves featuring popular Gothic and death metal singers. Robert turns off all the lights in the house and lights a lantern.

"It's better if the house is dim for this," he says. "I don't use candles except for rituals. Candles can be dangerous." He pops one of the CD's into his stereo and a strident metal sound issues from the speakers. "You ladies want some beer?" he asks.

"Beer?" Anika asks.

"Yeah, as a starter," Robert says.

"Sure," Antonio says, looking at the stakes on the wall with his finger on his chin.

Anika approaches him.

"I'm hungry," she says.

"Come here Antonietta, sit with me," Justine says, suddenly.

Antonietta looks at Antonio. Just like that, she seems to seek approval. Antonio smiles and nods at her. Antonietta goes and sits down with Justine.

"So long no see you," Justine says as Antonietta sits down.

Antonietta does not respond. She looks at Justine's throat with narrowed, sensual blue eyes.

"Look, I got this bracelet," says Justine. "My mother bought it for me. She thinks it'll match my dark clothes."

Antonietta suddenly looks at the bracelet. "It is beautiful," she says, her manners changing at this moment.

Antonio now walks into the kitchen.

Anika stands alone, watching Antonietta, Justine and Enrique. Enrique looks at her with love.

"Why don't you come join us?" he asks. He moves over to one side of the couch.

"Sure, why not?" Anika says. She comes over and sits down next to him.

"So, where are you from?" Enrique asks.

"How long have you been a vampire?" Anika asks.

Enrique laughs. "You didn't answer my question."

His laughter stops. Robert suddenly screams from within the kitchen. Many things pause within his being. He turns his eyes, quickly.

Robert is yelling, "Get the fuck away from me!"

Enrique and Justine shoot up to their feet, concerned, but are harshly brought back down by Antonietta and Anika, who immediately clamp their fangs on their necks. Justine screams as her neck is assaulted and pierced. Yet she finds away to tear herself. Her escape is brief—she falls instantly to the floor on her back. In almost less than a second, Antonietta is back on top of her. Now Justine has no escape. Antonietta has her pinned like a ton of bricks. Justine pushes against her body, but can barely move Antonietta now.

Antonio appears after a moment and looks at the scene. Antonietta seems to be making love to Justine's neck, lying upon her sensually. Justine's arms aid in the sensual image, going around Antonietta as if with desire. One of her hands, however, is gripping the back of Antonietta's dress, as if in a last attempt to dislodge her.

Antonio sees the end of the feeding. When Antonietta and Anika look at him, their chins are running with blood. Their fangs are long, and even now appearing hungry.

"Good job, my darlings," Antonio says. "Now, let us finish this task. We do not want these vampires to chase about our prey." He takes down the stakes from the wall and gives one to each of the girls. Then he goes into the kitchen to finish the job with Robert.

Antonietta is guided by Anika in the task of annihilating the threat of resurrection. Able to easily lift the four-hundred pound leaden lid of her casket, Antonietta is able to neutralize the threat of new vampires by impaling the stake in Justine's heart. After the task is done, the trio departs.

Antonietta feels the change as she flies with her new companions. She feels a little more wicked and dreamy. The hunt was not only satisfying, but also romantic.

"We must find a few more of these vampires," Antonio says as they fly. He's carrying Robert's lantern in his hand, and a number of unused stakes in his coat pockets.

"I would like to chase that with some alcohol," Anika says. "The night is young. And I took some money from Enrique."

"I'll put the lantern on a roof," Antonio says.

Antonietta feels fed, full, and is happier. In spite of her sadness a few hours ago, she can see her future now. She does not have to hunt alone, and Anika and Antonio are willing to share their blood with her. Even if that was not enough to give her a true sense of her new self, she sees no other way of surviving now. The change is coming over her slowly, and yet it is beginning to cling to her. She sees Antonio and Anika in a new light, both as providers and companions. The love she felt for and from Antonio's lips in her dreamy state, which did not make her fall love with him, is not something she could turn down without missing it already. She knows she has to give Anika something of herself as well. She knows the vampire was somewhat jealous as she and Antonio made love, though there wasn't much Anika could do about it. She was, and is, as locked into Antonio's world as she is now, and feels that neither could part from this center, even if the opportunity was given.

7

““My father used to say, 'if you get killed by a ghost, you become a ghost; if you get killed by a zombie, you become a zombie.' 'How was the first zombie made?' I asked him. 'It was a spell,' he said. So I am part of that spell. I hope he is right and that I'm not a fluke, and his stories not just stories. I hope my love is not a ghost wandering around somewhere. I would still be alone."

Engusanado stares at the small heap of earth on his grave. He has lit a candle to see his love better when she reappears. It was not an easy task lighting it. He wasted many matches before he got a flame going, since he is very awkward, except when capturing a worm. Engusanado lies down to wait, closing his eyes again.

"Soon," he says. "It can't be too long. I do not wish to light another candle."

Minutes later, a blistered hand comes through the mound as if looking for air. Then there is a desperate disruption of the mound as Joanna digs herself out. This resuscitates Engusanado. He gets up on his elbow.

He sees the woman he loves sit up, suddenly. Her hair is full of dust, and her face full of blisters. When she sees him, she breaks out of the grave and stands up as fast as she can. Engusanado also gets up, but he's in a good mood. He stretches his arms.

"Oh, my beauty," he says. "Love of my life."

Joanna rounds her eyes and stretches one of her blistered arms to stop him.

"No! Who are you! Get away from me!" she says, her voice hoarse.

Engusanado stops.

"But why?" he says. "I'm your husband, Arthur!"

"Arthur!" she says, still stepping back. "No, no! What a terrible nightmare!"

"Nightmare is what death has been without you, my love," Engusanado says.

Thinking that this is a dream, Joanna looks at him. Somehow, she is not afraid anymore.

"You are not the same you used to be," she says, suddenly. "But why am I talking to you? I will wake up soon. I have visitors to attend to. And you are wasting your time. I do not bed the dead!"

"But we are the same now, love," he says.

"The same! No, I will wake up! You will stay dead!" She backs away even more. "Someone, please, ring the bell! Oh, no! Did I set up the alarm? Oh, wake up, Joanna! Wake up!" She looks at her arms again. "No, I am beautiful!"

"You are, my pretty worm," Engusanado says. "Always have been. My dear Engusanada. I think that would be the right name for you."

Joanna rounds her eyes again. She moves further away.

"No, I will wake up soon," she says. She looks at her arms again. "Oh, terrible, terrible nightmare! I am still beautiful!"

"Yes, you are," Engusanado says. "Especially now. If you could only look in the mirror, you would know."

"No, I need to get back home," Joanna says. She sees the steps to the trapdoor and starts moving toward them, though slowly. The bottom of her satin gown has the stains of someone who went to the restroom and had no time to even lift up the skirt.

"Home is here now, my love," Engusanado says. Joanna is still walking to the steps. He follows her, also slowly, but with longer steps, until he is near her. "Come here."

Joanna turns and raises a fist. She is angry.

"Stop where you are, you worm-eaten carcass!" she says.

Engusanado slaps her. Joanna moans a cry and touches her face with her blistered hands. She looks at Engusanado with large, dead, dark eyes.

"What is this, my love?" Engusanado asks. "You want to kill me again? I dare you to try."

Joanna is still. She is now looking at Engusanado with fear.

"Come, there is no place to go," Engusanado says.

"Why did you do it?" she asks, realizing she is not waking up.

"To show you I am master now," Engusanado says.

Joanna looks at him a little longer, and drops to the floor.

She sits down and folds over with pain.

"Why do the dead feel pain?" she says.

"To show us that death is not the end," Engusanado says. He leans over her and strokes her back. "Oh, my love. How many new memories we will create."

Joanna feels more pain at hearing these words.

"Oh, but my manners!" Engusanado exclaims. "The hour of dinner has passed. Food may make you feel better. Stay here."

He gets up and goes up the steps.

Joanna stays down a little longer. When she realizes Engusanado is gone, she gets up and starts ascending the steps. She will leave, leave now! Outside the crypt, she sees the window. The moon is shining brightly. As she walks by the window, she sees a little of her image and turns to see it more fully. What one might not see with living eyes, she sees now with ones that, at least to the normal world, are dead. She screams and backs away, her blistered hands on her face.

She sits on the floor, wondering how all this came to be, why the dead came to hunt her. She gets up again after a moment, determined to end the nightmare, to be again what she used to be.

She walks slowly to the door, almost as if she was disabled. When she opens it and looks outside, something seems to stand before her—the wall of the dead, that which does not let us leave the grave. There is life outside this temple of death, yet the door is shut for her. She is unable to move forward. She turns and goes back down the steps to the candle-lit crypt. She lies down on the floor.

Sometime later, Engusanado returns. He has captured many worms. Even as Joanna sleeps, or seems to sleep, he puts the worms—as many as he can—into her mouth, as if that will revive her. Joanna feels the worms in her mouth and raises her head. She spits out the worms like they were dust, sits up, and backs away without getting up.

"What in the living world was that!" she exclaims.

"The dead world," Engusanado says. "It is dinner. You'll enjoy them. They're more plentiful after it rains." He picks up the worms that she spat out and takes her hand. "Come, try them. I know you're hungry. They're not bad at all. They're funny things. They love to wriggle in the mouth, like jesters."

Except through pride, Joanna feels no aversion to the worms. She takes them and puts some in her mouth, because she is hungry. It is a psychological hunger, not a real, living one.

As soon as the things start wriggling in her mouth, she starts to cry. Those may be the last remaining tears. She picks out the worms again, throws them on the floor, and leans over the ground. This is her life now. She is dead.

"Oh, what a waste," Engusanado says. "They might be offended now and won't taste as good." He picks up the discarded worms and puts them in his mouth. "Ah, very good," he says. "Seems the rich, plain flavor is still there. Do not worry, my love. You'll get used to them. We'll go hunting for them together. Our first adventure, aye? After the rains, they're all over the place, like fish. What does a king of Egypt have? Gold does not feed the dead. This is the dinner of the aristocrat. True, living worms!"

Albertini's eyes are open. Through some mysterious undead motor, he can move his head from left to right, but he can't walk it. The little animation allows him to look around, the only thing he can do. The rest of him is still. His body can do nothing without his head, and his head is stuck in one place without his body. His cellphone has been ringing for the last few days, but he hasn't been able to answer it. It is running out of battery, and no one has come to visit him.

He is also starving. It is a strange hunger. It seems like he is whole in spirit, but physically detached. His blood is all over the place, his heart in another part of the room. He's very disabled. If someone could put him back together, it would be his salvation. The light is still on in the room. It comes from a small lamp on a table. Albertini closes his eyes, but opens them again. Someone is knocking on his door with the door knocker.

"Albert! Antonietta!" he hears. "Are you guys in there? Why is no one answering the phone? Hello? Anyone in there?"

Sunset is about an hour away and the clear is departing. A face appears before the window. It is that of a young man who peeks between the curtains. It takes a minute of looking and inspecting before the voice sounds again.

"Shit! Shit!" Albertini hears. It is an alarmed voice.

Whoever is looking through the window has gone into a panic. After a little while, the window glass breaks. The young man steps in, still saying, "Shit! Shit! Oh, fuck!"

He saw Albertini's body on the floor through the window. As he climbs in between the broken glass, Albertini closes his eyes. The young man sees the entire scene and gets close to the Albertini's head.

"Oh, fuck, fuck! What happened here? Oh, shit! Shit! Shit!" He is crying madly as he runs to the door, opens it, and yells, "Help! Help! Somebody killed by brother!"

Half an hour later, several people look in mute horror at the house and the yellow tape across the street. An ambulance and a firefighter truck are parked near the house. Police cars occupy the entire length of the block. Detectives and police and people with cameras come in and out of the house. About an hour later, Albertini's parts are put on a stretcher, along with his heart, and put into the ambulance. Albertini goes along with it, keeping his eyes closed through the entire ordeal.

The news media calls Albertini's murder a brutal crime. Due to its nature police suspect it was one of passion, and that the person that committed it may have wounded and kidnapped Antonietta. The two separate spills of blood, several feet from each other, with no drops connecting them, reveal they may belong to different people.

The forensic analysis on Albertini's body takes only a couple of hours to complete. The manner of death is evident. The deceased's head was cut off, and his chest penetrated by some sharp device that allowed for the removal of his heart. The gun near Albertini's right hand indicates that Albertini tried to defend himself.

After the examination, Albertini is removed to another room, where his head is reattached by order of the Coroner so as to prepare him for his funeral. His heart is also returned. It is put in a bag and put inside his body, which is sewn back together. Then Albertini is taken to another room from where he will depart to another location for embalming, a process which will drain every last drop of blood from his body.

On day three Albertini is taken to the funeral home, where a woman will make him look attractive for service. The woman is alone with him. It is already evening and she is about to be done. New clothes are on Albertini. As the woman gets close to his face to apply makeup to his eyelids, Albertini's arm springs up.

He takes the woman by the back of her head and pulls her to him. His fangs clamp on her neck. There is no one to hear her scream, though the sound goes around the room in high pitched decibels. Albertini drains her. When he's done, he pushes her to the floor.

But he still can't get up and walk. He would be a useless walker if he tried. The blood is not touching his heart and giving feet. Instinctively, he undoes his shirt and the threads closing his chest. He puts his hand is his body and takes out the bag containing the heart. He tears the bag and inserts the heart back into his chest, his hand going through the space of his broken rib. The new blood allows the heart to reattach itself and to begin to pulse. It is very strong in the undead. But now there is a hole in his chest again. He covers it with his jacket.

In one hour, the undead energy has reattached his head to his body, naturally. The clamps in his neck intended to keep his head in place are doing their job. There are also stitches around the same area which orbit his neck like a form of choker, though they are concealed by the high collar of his shirt. But he lives now and he can get up.

In spite of this, he doesn't. He doesn't know what to do or where to go. He is alone and somewhat scared. With blood back in his body, he feels more lost than when he was just a head on the floor. His memory seems to have gone somewhat as well. He only knows he is angry and has a strong urge for revenge.

After some time, he finally sits up and looks around. He doesn't know where he is or where he should go from here. As he reflects and tries to put things back together, the woman wakes up and raises herself halfway from the floor. She has become a vampire. Albertini is taken aback, as if she appeared out of nowhere. They look at each other a moment, each studying the other. She seems lost. Both say nothing.

Albertini knows what she is and is surprised to see her, yet doesn't care much for her. Her blond hair, however, reminds him of someone. He looks in the distance, into the darkness and into the light. Antonietta! Suddenly, all comes back. He gets off the table and looks at the woman again.

The woman still looks at him. She never stops looking. She is confused.

"Goodbye," Albertini says.

He walks to the door in the distance. The woman follows him with her eyes. She will have to face her own death, alone.

As Albertini exits the door, he becomes aware of voices and people walking toward his location. He levitates to the ceiling. From there, he sees a man and a woman. The stop by the door, wondering why it is opened.

"Susan!" the woman yells.

When they are out of sight, he flies out of an open window. Once he is far enough, he descends and starts to walk. When he reaches the center of Magnolias, he hides, almost as if he fears people will attack him. He will be afraid of the world for a while. When he catches a prey, it will be from darkness, and only when he is hungry. He will know he must do it. That he *must* hunt. In time, he will be comfortable doing it.

This beginning is usual for lonely vampires who start on their own, without mentors, without someone leading them. It's not that a vampire needs to be led, since he moves by instinct. He knows what he wants. But he is cautious at first, and as afraid of the prey as the prey is of him. Eventually, he will get used to it. He will realize his power. Fewer than most start their undead adventure the way Anika and Antonietta started theirs.

Albertini, however, has something more than hunger for blood. He wants revenge. He remembers the night at Bloodwine. He remembers his girl. His Antonietta. The bastards killed his girl!

9

Around two in the morning, Antonio, Anika and Antonietta enter the mausoleum. Even before they enter the crypt, they see the light of the burning candle. Below, they see Engusanado has company.

Engusanado is talking to Joanna, who is refusing to do something.

"Come, it's time for bed," he says. "Wandering around is not a proper thing for a dead woman, when the daylight can catch you. Come, get in the hole."

"No!" Joanna says.

"Shall I put you in myself? Just like I did on our wedding night, when I got you into bed? Is that what you want?"

"Keep your hands away from me."

"Oh, come on, kiss me, be a darling."

"Stay away from me," Joanna says.

"Ah, you'll learn, you'll learn," says Engusanado. "Get in the hole!"

The three vampires laugh, though they show respect by being somewhat quiet. Joanna lies down inside the hole, though she is angry.

"Good, my darling," Engusanado says. "I might fit in yet, though it'll be a little tight. I'll protect you from the little eating bastards. You got too much flesh for their disdain, and you being so beautiful—more beautiful than ever—might tempt them even more."

Antonio raises his eyebrows, impressed. Engusanado is a romantic. Engusanado feels them at that moment and turns. "Oh, we have friends.

Here she is, as you see her," he says. "The killer of my heart, the life of my death."

"The killer," Anika murmurs, softly. She already detests the woman.

Joanna sits up at that moment. Antonio is handsome, and the women are beautiful. She looks at Engusanado and then at her blistered arms. She groans and voluntarily lies back into the hole, so she will see no more.

"She has tears left," Engusanado says. "Doesn't she cry beautifully? Tomorrow I have plans. We'll wander the garden together and fish out worms. Aye, we'll go fishing. You will love that, my love," he says to Joanna. "A little adventure."

Joanna cries even more, and more loudly.

"Well, it's time for us to go to sleep," Engusanado says. Still wearing Antonio's suit, he lies in the hole next to Joanna, and wraps his arms around her.

When he closes his eyes, Joanna is still crying somewhat. Antonio and Anika, however, do what they always do. They cover the grave with the earth. When that is done, they hear Joanna no more.

Then Antonio takes Anika and Antonietta's hands. He brings their bodies to him and puts an arm around each of them. He kisses Anika first and strokes Antonietta's back. He kisses Anika a long time, taking his lips to her chin and her throat. Then he turns to Antonietta. He looks into her eyes, deeply. Antonietta looks likewise into his, and then they kiss. Antonietta's hand reaches for Anika.

Anika feels the call and moves toward Antonietta and stands behind her. Her hands go around to take Antonietta's breasts, her mouth going to her neck with little bites and kisses. Antonio goes from Antonietta's mouth to her neck as well. Now Antonietta feels both mouths on her.

Food makes a human sleepy—blood makes a vampire a vessel of passion. Antonietta feels the sensual vitality. This vitality drives one of her hands toward Antonio and the other behind her toward Anika. She tugs on Anika's long dress and pulls it up.

In front of her, Antonio has grown to full measure in her hand. With both her hands at work, she leans her head back over Anika's shoulder.

The blood she has drunk has given her this present need. It's what allows a vampire not to feel alone, to have a purpose, since everything else is gone. Blood and sex are all a vampire has, plus an eternal dream.

Dare not to dream except for this, for other dreams are impossible and you'll have a lonely road ahead. Powerful vampires in castles feel the emptiness of chasing human ends after a while and always revert to their primal selves.

The vampires in this crypt answer to this primal call most fully. They have of each other, both in blood and the excretion that blood makes possible and that they taste with their tongues. At the end of the tryst, it's hard to tell who loved the other more.

Antonio does the honor of pulling up the leaden lid for both his immortal lovers and puts it back on once they lie down to sleep. Then he goes into his own casket, satisfied, pulls the lid closed, and closes his eyes.

Antonietta does not sleep for a while. Her eyes dart across the darkness of the closed casket like one seeking answers. Her feelings are not the same as they were before the nocturnal tryst in this room of the dead. There is a dark, frenetic and honest passion among these immortals, those who ended her life and who now seem to have rescued her. Her killers, her lovers. Also her companions. Yes, she remembers now, though in morsels—for she hasn't stopped trying to remember the pieces of her life—about her transformation.

Knowing them as she knows them now, as she knows herself now, she arrives at a moment of forgiveness. She is as much an animal as anything that ever thirsted for blood, regardless of how the transformation from human to animal occurred. She understands now.

The sex, the romance, blinded and awakened her. She gravitated to another universe. A glimpse through the curtain of memory now reminds her suddenly of Albertini, and how she used to feel under his body—or when she stretched up her form while she was the driver of her own pleasure and he a pawn beneath her. There was also much passion in that mortal love. Though she doesn't remember many things yet, she remembers this now. It is a form of success. Many newly-turned vampires take months to remember even vestiges of what they left behind, while she accomplisehd this in a matter of a few nights.

One of her hands is on top of the other over her chest, the same way her bed companion lays her hands. Anika had her hands that way when she was put in the casket the first time ninety-nine years ago. At that time, her hands held a flower. A few of the petals not turned to dust are still in the casket; the old stem in one corner.

While Antonietta misses the remembered fragments of her former life, she is now also aware of this one, even if the fruits are sour on contemplation when compared to all the suns she will no longer see. But that is the way for those who sink suddenly into darkness and yet get to live to see the moon. And what is better? To die young to enjoy the night, or to die old and have no chance at ever wandering around to enjoy the luxury of a breath that does not dampen a glass?

At least this is the thought of the undead, for the living do not wish to live forever. But for a vampire a stake is always in the offing, and if one gets tired of the false breath, one might voluntarily offer oneself to it. If not, one can take a saunter up a hill at dawn, or take a dive into the fire.

Finally Antonietta closes her eyes and goes to sleep.

10

The air is muggy around Grand Central Station, and Anika Lenbach cannot wait to get home. The white Edwardian hat with the ostrich plume is making the top of her head sweaty, and the silk chemise under her fine muslin—which she prefers over the constraining hobble attire seemingly designed as much to show her form as to trip and fell her should she undertake a little run across the thoroughfare—seems to be making a lake of her body. Neither her head nor her northern patience are made to stand this weather, even as she softens her features to display the wares of upper class fortitude. Perhaps she is the only woman fretting in New York with a smile, and the only one in fine muslin with a servant who is dressed as if for a cotillion.

It is obvious by his address, "Miss, it's best if we don't hasten. Manners, madam," that in terms of rank he is more an old, family butler than a helot, or an ancient English villein—a feudal subject who paid his master for his shackles in return for a bit of land.

He carries a small trunk in his right hand, imprinted on the front with the name *Shwayder* in small letters, and an umbrella on his left. At the thoroughfare, Anika raises her hand to a roofless motor cab at that moment just turning the corner. On it is a man with a small, thick mustache, who surveys her even as he approaches. This is not the only thing he does that gets Anika's attention. When he stops, he jumps off in a hurry and extends his hand to help her up to the front seat.

Anika accepts without much thinking of refusing the offer, and gets on. She puts her own umbrella between her legs and her pretty little handbag on her laps.

"Twenty-One Dominique, please," says the butler, putting himself, the trunk and his umbrella in the back seat.

On the way, the driver wipes his face with a handkerchief and then looks at Anika. He does it enough times to get Anika's attention. Anika notices his wandering eye, and slides some inches farther from him.

"Twenty-One Dominique," the driver says. "I know the place very well."

Anika only nods, and looks before her again.

"You know?" the driver continues. "I only drive this cab to pass the time."

Anika frowns, first for being addressed, second because she doesn't know why it is important for her to know the personal details of his life. However, she feels like she ought to answer.

"Do you get paid for it?"

"I do," he says.

"Then it's not just a pastime."

The driver is shocked. He laughs.

"Did you just arrive from the country?" he asks.

Anika is angry again.

"Do you get paid for information?" she asks.

"No, I'm just being friendly. Dominique Street is twenty minutes away, and I hate silence."

"Maybe you ought to change your pastime," she says.

The driver is stunned again, and laughs.

"Stop here," Anika says.

"Stop?" the driver exclaims. "But we're only a few minutes away."

"Will you overrule your passengers' wishes?"

"No, of course not," says the driver. He stops and Anika gets off. The butler doesn't question his mistress and starts picking up the trunk and his umbrella.

"Leave those there, George," Anika says. "We are merely changing seats."

"Yes, madam," George says.

The driver looks at her with calm shock and round eyes.

George gets in the front seat. Anika gets in the back on her own.

They arrive at Twenty-One Dominique. Several feet from the gate is a two-story mansion. A male servant is at the gate to receive them.

"Miss Lenbach, it's good to see you," he says, taking the trunk from the butler, who stays outside to settle the fare.

The driver looks as Anika enters the gate, even as George puts the money in his hand. After paying, George goes to the gate. He does not go in. He stands with his back against it, and nods to the driver.

The driver nods back and drives away.

"Is Mother home?" Anika asks the servant.

"Yes, madam. She is with company at the moment, your cousin William. I was almost not here to receive you. Your mama received your telegram only an hour ago."

"An hour ago?" Anika exclaims. "It's this heat. Nobody wants to work, except the wrong sort."

An elegant woman is in the parlor with a young man, drinking tea. It is William, who immediately gets up when he sees Anika. He is blond and very boyish-looking, though he is nearly thirty.

Anika brightens up and runs to him.

"William!" she says.

"My dear cousin," William says. He wraps his arms around her and then moves away to look at her. "But you look delightful!"

"Oh, it took you long enough to compliment me," Anika says.

"As you know, I've been away for two months," William answers.

"Exactly, two months," Anika says.

William laughs.

"I beg your pardon. No gentleman ought to wait two months to compliment a lady. Especially his cousin."

"Third cousin, dear cousin."

"Indeed, the fact makes it more imperative," William says. "No one ought to compliment close relations. It's against etiquette."

"Well, and is mother not to have a compliment from her daughter?" says the lady at the parlor.

Anika turns.

"Oh, Mama, of course. I've missed you."

Mother and daughter embrace.

"How was the country?" Mrs. Lenbach asks.

"Oh, insupportable," Anika says. "It's too bad when people divorce.

I thought it was illegal. But Papa, if you want to know, is well."

"I'm glad to hear it," says Mrs. Lenbach.

"He sends you his regards, and hopes you got the flowers he sent you last week. I told him, 'Papa, one ought not to send flowers such a long way, they wilt, and it's no compliment. Mama might think you're sending a secret stab…I mean, message."

"Well, I did receive them," says Mrs. Lenbach. "They're in the garden."

"Oh? Where?"

"All over."

Anika turns with a smile.

"Well, my dear William. Now that you're acquainted with my parents' happiness, how about a little turn among the thorns—I mean, flowers?"

William looks at Mrs. Lenbach.

"Don't let me detain you," Mrs. Lenbach says. "I'm sure you and your cousin—*third* cousin—have much to say to each other."

William and Anika do not enter the garden, but stand against the balustrade of a large stone deck overlooking it.

"It's good to see you," William says. "I was afraid to miss you."

"Afraid to miss me? Why so funereal?" Anika says.

"Well, as you know, I'm a lieutenant in the Army and… Well, two days ago I received an order from my commanding officer to present myself at the Mexican border. I'm sure you've heard people talk about the conflict happening there."

"No, I try to keep them out of earshot," Anika says.

"Well, there is a war on the other side, if you must know," William says. "Threatening our security and our greed."

"War! I thought they were all ended."

"Indeed they have not. Anyway, I was afraid to…"

"To…"

"To miss you," he says.

Anika looks at him.

"Well, you didn't miss me."

"No, I am braver now that I see you."

Anika looks away to the garden.

"Are you staying here tonight?" she asks.

"If your mother does not object, I wouldn't mind spending my last day here."

"Why not with your parents?" Anika asks.

"My parents…They already gave me their blessings."

"And now you want mine."

"No, I was hoping at least for a benediction."

"Well, have good travels," Anika says.

William laughs.

"I will miss you, indeed," he says.

"I *do* wonder why you came here to spend your last day," Anika says.

"You were the closest place in town," William says.

"The Plaza Hotel is closer to your parents'."

"But their flowers are not very pretty."

"Ours have thorns," Anika says.

"Indeed," William says, almost laughing. "But really…I came here for another reason."

"What is it?" Anika asks.

"To…To say goodbye to you." He looks at her, deeply.

Anika looks back at him.

"What makes you think I want to say goodbye?" she says.

William smiles and turns to the garden.

"I'm glad to hear you say you don't wish to say goodbye," he says.

In the evening, in his guest bedroom, William thinks of Anika. He is madly in love with her.

"Coward!" he says. "But it is best. Should something happen to me…Why should I condemn you? It's better to wait, and when I return, if I return…"

He digs into his pockets and takes out a little box. He sets it down on the bed and opens it. The lantern on the bedside table reveals a ring. He strokes the ring with his finger.

"When I return," he says.

He is so deep in thought, he does not hear his door open.

"Why did you not tell me?" he hears.

He looks up. Anika is standing in the soft ligh, wearing a sleeping gown.

William closes the ring box.

"I wanted to wait," he says.

Anika looks at him a moment, then turns to the door.

William thinks she's going to leave and gets up, but Anika only closes the door. He sits back on the bed. Anika approaches him. He is about to get up again, but Anika pushes him down.

An hour later, they are in each other's arms.

"Shouldn't we have waited until we were married?" he asks.

"There are times when things cannot wait," Anika says.

William reflects on the words and smiles.

"Maybe you are right," he says. "But I hope to return. We'll throw a great ball. I'd like to see you in that fabulous red dress."

"Will I be wearing the ring then?"

William thinks a moment. He reaches for the ring box on the bedside table.

"After tonight, I think you should be wearing it," he says. He pulls the ring off the box and slips it on her finger.

Anika embraces him and kisses him.

"What would your mother think if she knew what we did?" he asks a moment later. Anika's head is on his chest.

"Lovers hold secrets," Anika replies. "And besides, should we depend on the opinions of others, even that of our own parents? When life throws so many things your way, so many uncertainties, it's a shame—no, a sin—to waste the moment that offers happiness, even if it is brief."

William smiles. He kisses her blond hair. "My dear, dear Anika!"

Anika closes her eyes.

"How did you learn about my reason for being here? William asks as he strokes her head. "Did Mama spill something?"

"Mother told me in a way that seemed Chinese to me. I had to translate it on my own."

William laughs.

"I didn't know love could make a man a coward," she says. "And a man who is a soldier!"

"You are right. Bullets don't scare a man, but being rejected by the woman he loves, the woman of his dreams, does."

"Am I the woman of your dreams?" Anika asks.

"Yes, all of them."

"All of them!" Anika exclaims with humor.

"All the ones you can think of," William says. "If you can think of one dream, you are in it. Think of a million—well, we'll have to rush to get to all of them, but we'll do it together. How can half of a person walk into a place meant for a whole one?"

Anika laughs and kisses him. They lie silently for a moment. Then Anika turns her eyes to the window. "Do you notice how the moon has lingered in the same place for an hour?" she asks. The drapes on the window are open. The moon in the sky is full and large. "At least it seems so."

"She's a spy," William says.

"At least she's a beautiful spy, and tells no secrets," Anika says. "Sometimes, in my moments of melancholy, when I'm outside in the garden, she seems to be on fire. Yet she only sends down a soft, silver glow. Not enough to see where you're going. Unless I have a bad sight."

"She shines enough for lovers to see each other," William says; "and low enough to be quiet. It is a light for lovers."

Anika smiles and kisses his shoulder.

"I wonder what it would be like to be on it and do on it what we just did in bed," she says.

"It probably would be cold," William replies. "One day we might cross the ocean of the sky and find out."

"If we could fly there, at least far enough to be close to it," Anika says.

A month later, a letter arrives. William is dead. It breaks all of Anika's dreams. The end of something that seemed within reach of a hand throws her into a vast depression. It's hard to keep her composure at the funeral, especially at sight of William's face in the open casket. He is still. He doesn't speak. He doesn't smile. It is hard not to throw herself over the casket. Her veil barely conceals her tears. She receives condolences because she was his betrothed.

Anika keeps William's ring on her finger. She kisses it every night with tears in her eyes.

For a week after the funeral, a Model T, dresssed as a cab, is seen passing by the mansion. It happens every day, yet the driver never has any passengers. The last time it is seen down that road is in the evening, when Anika and George get in it.

Anika is on her way to see her father again, who sent her a telegram saying he is ill. The driver is wearing a dark hat and a scarf across his face.

After half an hour driving, the cab stops near a forest. When it drives away again, it leaves something behind against a tree: the body of George. The old man has a bullet in his head. Anika is still in the cab. The driver is the man of nearly two months ago, the inquistive cab driver.

As midnight arrives, they approach a small, eerily quiet town. As he begins to slow down, Anika opens the vehicle's door and jumps out. She runs through a wooded area to a house not far away. It is an abandoned house, nestled between factory buildings, all closed and dark.

When she sees the lights of the Model T, she runs again and turns the corner. She finds a house with an open gate. The driver saw her turn the corner, and he follows. He drives around the block. He doesn't see her anywhere and pulls up a few feet from a tree. He gets out of the vehicle as quickly and silently as he can and bends over outside his car door to shut off the acetylene gas that lights his headlights. Then he goes to the front to blow off the wick. The whole act is accomplished in less than a minute. Then he walks around to try to find her.

11

Antonietta is asleep when Anika gets out of her casket and opens Antonio's. Antonio looks at her.

"Has a bad dream disturbed your sleep?" he asks.

"Perhaps," Anika says. "Or it is a nightmare dressed as a dream."

Antonio sits up.

"How can I relieve your soul of that bad dream?" he asks.

"I'll show you," Anika says.

Antonio gets out. Anika kisses him.

"You are full of passion," Antonio says. "Is it just you and me this time?"

"Yes," Anika says. "I will share my skin but not my love."

"To some mortals, it is the same thing."

"Not to a dead woman, and hopefully not to a dead man."

"If you fear, be at ease, my love for you has no bounds. It can neither be replaced nor shared."

"Until now I have believed that."

"Do you not still believe?" Antonio asks.

"I do enough to be able to convince me that I want to do more than what I have done so far."

"Tell me your dreams," Antonio says.

"My dream is to waste no more time and to live something I have always wanted to live. Back in the days of my life, it was just a dream.

Today, it seems possible."

Antonio smiles, even as he looks at her in wonder.

"The moon is glorious today, even a vampire can tell," Anika says. "Come with me." She takes Antonio's hand and leads him up the steps. The moon outside the window is bright, but it has risen. Anika leads Antonio out the door.

"What now?" Antonio asks when they're outside.

"Come up with me," Anika says. "Let us go up as high as we can."

"Are the stars reachable even for a vampire?" Antonio asks.

"We are not going to them," Anika says. "But near enough that we can feel we can touch them."

They rise toward the starry heavens, holding hands. They get very high, so high that, except for some patches of light, the world seems to disappear. They pass through clouds. The stars are truly visible at this height. The wind is strong and pushes on their clothes.

Over the last of the clouds, Anika lifts her dress.

"Oh, what a dream!" Antonio says.

Even for them the wind is cold and strong. Soon, Antonio's pants are undone. As they drop, however, they fall off his feet and fly away. They kiss with passion and hold onto one another. Anika sees a shooting star cross the sky.

As they embrace, Antonio tilts Anika back and lowers the top of her dress. His fingers go under and his tongue goes in her mouth. Anika renders a similar service between his naked legs. As a cloud approaches them, Antonio lowers himself, still holding onto her, and goes under her dress with his mouth.

When he gets up, he presses her body to his. As the cloud gets nearer, his hips move against her. Anika claws his back and bites him on the shoulder. They share each other's blood and, as they do, moving against each other, they shake. The cloud covers them.

When they descend to the garden, they kiss again with sweet kisses.

"I never knew, dead as I am, that I could ever experience a feeling such as I have experienced today," Antonio says.

"I never thought I could remember a dream so dear," Anika says. "But now that I have lived it, close the coffin, never let me out again!"

"Ah, I would not like to do that. I rather have this feeling again. It will be always new."

Anika smiles. Holding his hand, they return to the mausoleum and back down the steps to the burial chamber. The wick of the candle is still going, but the candle is eaten away.

"Tomorrow night, or whenever we wake up, we might share that dream again," Antonio says.

"Yes, I agree, it will never get old," Anika says. "I want to do it a thousand times."

"Indeed," Antonio says. "Now, let us look for something for me to wear." He looks into the suitcase and brings out a new pair of pants.

"Now my sleep will have a new dream," he says, once he is inside them. "Never did mortal live such a dream. If he did, he'd die, because he can't fly."

"He has invented airplanes," Anika says, and kisses him again. "Who knows that he may have invented things to stay suspended in the air without falling?"

"The blasts would prevent him from staying in one place without rolling about in the heavens like a cheerful tumbleweed. His body is too weak."

"But his passion strong when set on a purpose."

"You have respect for you meal," Antonio says, laughing.

"What's not to respect of a dog that can hide his bone in the backyard, or of a weasel that can take on a cobra, or a beaver who can build castles in water?"

Antonio laughs.

"My love for you has no bounds," he says, and kisses her. "Goodnight, Sweet Love. May your dreams be ever filled with things that don't haunt the dead man's night."

Anika gets back into her casket and closes the lid.

Outside, the night clears and turns to day.

At noon, two men arrive to the gate of the cemetery. One of them is Abel Mathias, the owner of a funeral home, and the other John Alexios, the CEO of a company that runs cemeteries.

"It is such an old cemetery," says John.

"You say you want to start using it again?" Abel asks.

"Yes. And we want to fix it up. It's a historical site. Some of the graves are two, even three hundred years old."

"I wonder why it was forgotten," says Abel.

"People die," John says. Then he laughs. "I don't think it was forgotten. I know of people that come here sometimes. Kids. Some of them have disappeared."

"The dead took 'em," Abel says, laughing.

"Who knows?" John says, shrugging. "There were no traces of them around here."

"Interesting," Abel says. "So when do you start work?"

"When we get the city permit," John replies.

"I see. And are you going to fix that mausoleum back there?"

"Yeah. It's an old family mausoleum. I suspect it's dusty and dirty inside. We want to go down there and clean it up. It has a basement with an old crypt. No one has gone in there in years."

"Well, let me know when you're ready to start working," says Abel. "I'll put it on my fliers. When you start getting ready to bury people, I'll put it on the website as our official cemetery."

"Yeah, you get five percent for every confirmed referral," says John.

"Very good," Abel replies.

They look at the cemetery a little longer and walk away.

12

Vampires are social organisms who hate loneliness and competition. They possess the instinct of the lion, who makes sure the soil of his little kingdom only feels his paws and those of his females and cubs. Now a vampire, Albertini is sensible of this dichotomy. He also prizes secrecy and the importance of being part of a short supply of vampires. Too many vampires betray, not by their existence, but by their numbers, the concealment in which they operate. Secrecy is a commodity. Once a world gets used to the "things that are out there," regardless how terrifying, it will adapt to the new ways. And since the living operate in both daylight and nighttime, and vampires sleep in the day, it is better not to lift the lid of the coffin for public view.

The knowledge of this danger is innate to vampires, whether they can put words to the fear or not. They sense it, and devise ways to feed and to stay hidden. This drives vampires to work often alone, even as they seek companionship, a place to belong.

Albertini is still a little weak from having all his blood removed by the embalming. The girl he drained at the funeral parlor gave him just enough to sustain him, but now he needs more of the life-giving substance, at least an extra liter to satisfy his remaining need. He had not drunk to conquer the soul or the heart, but to feed.

Vampires who like slaves and lovers, the warm, living sensation of voluptuous lips, drain their victims slowly and passionately. That creates the bond between master and slave, and among those who'd become lovers, the fulcrum, the passion and the fire in their undead life. Accidental encounters happen, and sudden transformations, such as the one he caused upon the girl at the funeral home, and the one Antonio and Anika caused upon his Antonietta. The love that would come gradually is annulled by such quickness, and the slave or lover is harder to retain under the spell.

Albertini doesn't know, however, that not all is written in stone in the vampire world, and that love can be kindled, though slowly, even among vampires who see each other for the first time, because the need of belonging is as strong as the fear of being alone.

At this moment, Albertini is too angry to think of passion. He only thinks of revenge and finding more blood. Yet he is cautious. First of all, he needs a place to go into before dawn.

He wanders, partially on foot and partially in the air. In a dense wood a mile from town, he comes across a hole under a tree. He tests it. It fits him. However, it offers no concealment from the world or the sun. He tries to find, in his foggy brain, a more propitious location, and casts himself to the air.

He stays distant from the city lights and descends into a neighborhood. He looks around. Though dark, there are too many lights. Too much humanity. In the daytime, he is the prey. There is no safety here, and no place to hide.

He keeps moving. More lights below. He descends into darkness again. He lands in a cemetery. It is a unanimous vote against it. There is no place to rest there. Mourners go into mausoleums, and even if they didn't for one day, the doors to get inside would be locked, and a vampire can't sleep by a grave. The sun will eventually go up.

Next he flies by his old house. He lands a few meters away and walks toward it like a normal man. He stops across the street near a tree. From there he espies his old place. Lights are on in the house and police tape around the front lawn. A patrol car is stationed in front of it, with two policemen inside, one of whom is looking into some papers with a flashlight.

Albertini returns to the wooded area and finds the tree with the hole again. He gathers some brush and brings it to the hole. He enters feet first, lying on his stomach, and covers the hole with the brush. This will do, he thinks. He exits some time later. It is about an hour before dawn, the right time for what he intends to do.

He flies as quickly as he can toward the center of Magnolias. He lands on a high building and looks below. There are no passersby. He waits about fifteen minutes before returning to the hole, where he goes in as before and covers the entrance with the brush.

Just as he is about to sleep, he hears a noise. The brush stirs. His hand shoots out with lightning speed. It captures a large rat. He barely looks at it before its neck is in his mouth. He sucks its blood, piercing the furry skin with his incisive fangs. After feasting on it, he tears it in half and discards it.

He exits the hole and walks some distance down a declivity. He hears the sound of water. He soon discovers a small creek. On the other side is a large boulder. It is just ten minutes before the sun begins to kiss heaven's edge.

With undead strength, he carries it to his hole. He slides in again and pulls in the stone until the top touches the bottom of the tree above. The boulder becomes a door. Just as the sun breaks into the woods, Albertini goes to sleep.

Now that he has found a shelter, Albertini feels more at ease. By the evening, the fears of the night before have also eased. He swallows what remains, contemplating Magnolias lights from one of the trees in the little forest. He has a desire to be part of the world again, not believing he is dead, or refusing to. With some caution still, he takes to his wings.

Once in the town, he hides behind a trash bin in an alley. He tries bravery after a while. He adjusts his jacket and raises his face. His first look at the world outside the alley, however, makes him realize his change.

The world has become a hunting stage and those around are buffaloes and gazelles, and he is a lion, and still a little hungry. He raises his eyes to the sky as if he needs its great openness to breathe.

He has also become a thief. Back in the alley, before he hid behind the trash bin, he spotted a young man smoking a cigarette. Albertini watched him for a while.

The young man caught his glance after a moment and froze. He felt he was seeing a specter. Albertini had bright eyes.

Albertini walked to the light under which the young man stood. The small light wiped the brightness off his eyes, but he said nothing.

The man, however, continued looking at him as if he was seeing an apparition, but getting the best of himself, he asked, "Do you…Do you want a cigarette?"

Albertini simply nodded.

The man held out his pack and his lighter. The moment Albertini had them in his hand, he ran away with them.

The young man was stupefied a moment, and then crossed himself. He had just been robbed, but the speed of Albertini, who disappeared in a run—who was a something and then a nothing in an instant—caused him such a feeling of terror that he knew of no other thing to do.

Initially, Albertini had seen the young man as prey, and that made him fear him, because he could not accept what he was seeing, what he was feeling. Now walking the streets, Albertini smokes and sends a plume of smoke to the stars.

The simple act has a psychological effect. It makes him feel he is a part of the sphere. He begins to walk calmly among the herd, a little smile here and there in acknowledgement of a neck—just before he looks at the face—all dapper in his burial clothes, though the jacket is soiled from sleeping on the ground.

He doesn't feel he has to hide, an unreal belief in a town that knew him. A few people look at him as if they recognize him, but walk away only shaking their heads.

The news of his brutal murder—and now the disapearance of his body from the funeral home and that of the mortuary technician—has been all over the papers, especially in *The Magnolias Times*. In spite of this, Albertini doesn't see himself as an abnormal figure, though he can't mingle with the crowd as he would have a few days ago. Though his head was cut off, he is still upright, and moving around like the most alive person that ever walked Magnolias Blvd.

He knows he is a vampire and that he thirsts for blood, and that the people around, who don't bother him, are prey. Yet in his mind, he is only transformed, not dead. Perhaps if he knew—if he felt this was a dream—he would lie down in his grave and die. But most dead who survive complete darkness don't accept, believe, or know that they are dead.

A young woman in a black, funereal dress walking out of a café with a man spots him. Her eyes get so round, her irises swim in the very center of her sclerae.

"You are dead!" she says, stopping by him.

"Doth know Death?" Albertini asks, looking at a thing he'd like to have for dinner.

The man beside her laughs.

"What in the fuck!" he exclaims. "Hey, Albertini is alive!" he cries out loud. He raises his hands and dances around. "The motherfucker is alive!"

"Is this a fucking joke?" the young woman exclaims. She slightly retreats with her hands on her mouth. Then her hands drop. "Do you know who the fuck I am?" she asks, because Albertini does not seem to know her.

Albertini looks carefully at her, trying to remove the fogs from his memory.

"I'm your fucking sister!" she cries. Her eyes begin to swim in a pool of tears.

People gather around them, asking questions, looking at him.

"Holy shit!" some say. Others laugh.

Albertini backs away as if from buffaloes, as hands that could be horns begin to touch him.

"I have to go," he says. He turns and begins to run. He disappears.

His sister cannot believe what she just saw.

"What the fuck was that!" her companion exclaims.

Albertini's sister opens her mouth in shock. She sits on the floor.

"Who saw that?" her companion asks the crowd. "That wasn't real. Are we all high, or was it just me?"

"I fucking saw that," a young man replies.

"Ok, I'm going to church tomorrow," a woman says with finalty. "This is ridiculous." She walks away shaking her head.

"Roselin, come on."

Albertini's sister hears the words, but she can't move. She keeps looking in the distance.

"Roselin," her companion repeats.

Roselin sees a hand before her.

"Come on, I think we're all high," her companion says. "Or your brother is the greatest prankster that ever lived."

"His body disappeared from the funeral home," she says, softly.

13

On day six of her death, Joanna wakes up alone. Engusanado, still wearing Antonio's suit, is looking at her from a chair. It's one of the chairs from upstairs that he hauled down to the crypt. Among the items in the suitcase, which he opened again, he found a hat, and he is wearing it. He even managed to cross his legs. The new lantern Antonio brought is at his feet. With his pose and the suit, something of the old days seems to have returned to his death-marred face. He is an elegant zombie.

Joanna sits up and looks at him with wonder.

"Someone told me once, I remember," Engusanado says; "that killers ought not to die happy or have happy deaths. But I realize that he never considered that I would live with one of them. I think clearly now in my old, dead brain, and I've come to the conclusion that to make your death a misery is to make my death a misery, especially when we ought to share the same grave. I think death is punishment enough for you.

"It is your punishment, too, that you should spend eternity with the man you did not love. That's the reason you killed me. And I know why you did not love me. It is the same thing that led you to kill me. We do not kill dreams, not with a knife or with poison, unless we kill the dreams inside ourselves. It was a great deal my fault. I was weak. I was not a man. I was not weak because I loved too much. I was weak because I was not a man, and women want a man, a man to respect, who loves them and whom they can also love. A man that only the state can destroy, and not the whimsical things of life. A Napoleon. A Julius Caesar. Even Mark Anthony, who loved Cleopatra, was not destroyed by his love, but by Rome!

"Yes, some men have that. I never had that. Not that type of strength. A woman does not destroy something that by its mere existence brings her glory and a good home with servants, even if those servants are the man's own hands, and her glory the thought that others do not possess the wealth she has in him. No, I did not have the wealth of a masculine man, the man that only the state can destroy, whose existence means glory to the one who holds his arm. I only had a house, and a decent amount of money. It wasn't me who made you happy, but the money you could get from me. You would have never killed a man you loved."

"Old memories!" Joanna responds. "What matters now that we're both dead, and that thanks to you, not me? I did not walk into my own room and strangled myself to death. Do not think I don't know. Dead, I could still be a nurse. I just don't know how to heal the dead."

Engusanado realizes he made a mistake. Words cannot a penetrate a heart of steel, especially one that died without repentance. He philosophizes that the dead, except those who don't rise again, bring their essence into the grave.

"They die as they lived," he says to himself.

"Ha?" Joanna asks.

"I made a mistake," Engusanado replies. "But it makes no difference now. We'll make do." He cocks his head. "There is rain. Good day for hunting and fishing in the muddy ponds." He looks at Joanna with a smile. "Are you hungry, my love?"

Joanna crunches her old, dead, blistered face. "Are we having worms again?"

"What else do the dead eat, unless you're a vampire?" Engusanado says.

The mention of the soft-faced, soft-skinned and elegant vampires is a painful reminder of how she is so much different. "Too soon you came," she says. "And so inopportune, just as I was sleeping. But you never had any manners."

"Would you have preferred me showing up at one of your parties, and have your friends watch me strangle you to death?"

"Brutal man!" Joanna exclaims. She looks toward Anika's casket.

"Had I known what was going to happen, I would have gone hunting for vampires and presented my neck willingly before your death-eaten claws got anywhere near me. I would gladly have died and awakened in a chamber full of darkness and full of death, but beautiful still."

"Ah, your punishment is then greater than I thought," Engusanado says. "You say I did this to you. Would I have done it if I had died not knowing what closed my eyes? I do not believe ignorance chooses hell, but the one who commits a crime is dually responsible for his death and his hell."

"So this was revenge," Joanna says.

"It was something. I can't tell. I couldn't help it," Engusanado replies. "I had to see you. I did not plan to kill you, just see you. Perhaps have you see me. Fill you with guilt. Maybe regret. That would have been my revenge. My death-eaten hands acted from sudden anger, but also from deep love, for I still wanted to be with you, because I had forgiven you. Oh, what dead forgives? As much a coward in death as in life. My punishment is yet to live alone. But I forgive myself if no one else will. What a feeling to say that! One should always forgive oneself, but only if one is to change the path. I feel better already. Perhaps this is not the end for me. If I hope, I may rise from this grave and go to a better place, even if it is just a peaceful obscurity. And peaceful obscurity will bring a new birth. One can't be born again unless one dies, truly dies." He pauses a moment and then strikes his legs. "Well, how about them worms? I'll bring some to fill your pretty mouth."

When he retires, Anika and Antonietta's casket opens. Anika comes out. She sees the old, dead woman sitting in Engusanado's grave and gives her a mean look.

Joanna frowns. Then she sees Anika slip off her red dress and dig into the suitcase at her feet. Anika's skin and figure are beautiful even in death. Her back has no scar from death's lash. It is almost pristine and young and soft. But it is also cold. Joanna looks at her arms and her legs.

Anika pulls out one of Antonietta's short black dresses and slips it on.

"I feel your presence," says Antonietta, opening the casket Anika closed. She sits up and looks at Anika.

Anika turns to her. "Then the bond has grown," she says. "When you fear, you feel a presence, but also when you love. If you don't care one way or the other, you can sleep an eternity without anyone waking you up."

"I feel love," Antonietta says. "At least a dream that I love."

Antonio sits up in his casket.

"Then I also love," he says; "if that is the measure. Fear would not make me sit up but stand."

Soon they all look at Joanna, though they don't speak with her.

Joanna sees them embrace, laugh and kiss, then go, hand in hand, up the steps in their elegant clothes. She lies back down inside the hole, depressed.

Engusanado is outside in the garden, hunting for worms. The vampires appear, laughing. Then they fly up into the sky. He looks up a moment until they disappear. There are worms moving in his hand. He continues hunting. Not long after, he feels a presence. Standing, watching him, is Joanna.

"Aye, you'll get wet," he says. "Though it's only a drizzle now. When I came out, I felt like the rain would soak my very soul."

Joanna is frowning and crossing her arms. Then she looks at the ground. She bends down and picks up a worm.

"Ah, you found one," Engusanado says. "Come, there are more on this side. Too many to hold in one hand. But two hands? We need one to pick them up." Joanna approaches him.

"Right here, love, right here," says Engusanado.

Joanna looks down again. She bends over and picks up another worm.

"Oh, that is a fat one!" Engusanado says. "Might give us a skin yet."

14

One in the afternoon. The window is open behind the couch where Chad sits with a guitar. Sitting on the floor are Martin and Susan, a blond girl.

"Any vampire that fucked with you would be a dead man," Chad says, playing some strings.

"Aren't vampires already dead?" Martin asks.

"Yeah, think!" Susan tells Chad.

Chad throws himself back on the couch and laughs.

"But really," Susan says. "They hang out at Bloodwine. They think they're real vampires."

"That's sad," Martin says.

"But they don't all take themselves that seriously. I met one in the saloon. That's what they call it, where they all hang out. He was thinking quite clearly."

"He probably didn't have money for drugs," Chad says.

"Maybe," Susan says, laughing. "He said he was a vampire for fun. But he had a friend who had sharpened his canines. He started hitting on me."

"Yum, Susan the vampire!" Martin laughs.

"He kept staring at my boobs," Susan laughs. "At some point, I asked him: 'Shouldn't you be staring at my neck?' He laughed his ass off. But, yikes, I wouldn't be caught dead with him."

"They like blondes in the vampire world," Chad says, fingering the strings very quietly.

"Not in the movies. They like brunettes," Susan says.

"Underworld!" Martin exclaims.

"I love that movie," Susan says. "The second one, they kind of changed the story, though."

"Yeah, they did," Martin says. "But it was still cool, I think. Were the people at Bloodwine dressed up like in Underworld?"

"I guess," Susan says. "Typical Gothic style. And fake fangs." She laughs.

"Were they scared at your crucifix?" Chad asks, laughing.

"My necklace?" Susan laughs. "Not really. But I went to one of them and asked him, 'So, if I wanted to kill you, I would need a stake?' He came close to my ear and said: 'I want to put my stake in you.' He was very romantic." Martin throws himself back onto the floor with laughter.

It is three hours before Susan starts her evening shift at the funeral home, where she works from five to ten. She looks at her watch and says,

"I only have two hours to hang out."

"You make good money working with the dead?" Martin asks.

"It's a living," Susan says and looks at him. "See what I did there?"

Martin doesn't get it, but then he laughs. "Oh, right!"

"I think any dead that woke up would have a miserable time with you," Chad says.

"What do you mean?" Susan says. "I'm not mean. It'd tell him to go back to sleep."

Both Martin and Chad laugh.

"You don't get scared at night?" Martin asks.

"No," Susan replies. "In the beginning I kind of was scared about touching them. But you breathe in and out and then you can manage it. You get used to it. You also get to treasure life a little more."

"I see," Martin says. "Hey Chad, mind if I get another cold one?"

"Sure, you gonna have to buy a replacement, though."

"I'm only on my fifth," Martin says. "I don't even feel piss-like." He gets up and goes to the kitchen, opens the refrigerator, and then one of the cupboards. "Hey, you got brandy?" he yells.

"Yup," Chad yells back.

"Mind if I help myself?"

"Go ahead. Don't drink it all, though."

"I won't," Martin replies. He returns to the living room with a glass half-filled with brandy and a can of beer that he's already sipping. After an hour, he stops paying attention to the conversation, and falls asleep on the floor.

Susan, wearing a short, light, sky-color dress, gets on Chad's legs.

"People are going to watch from the street," Chad says.

Susan looks at his blue eyes, and massages his dark hair.

"Let them watch," she says. She pulls down the top of her dress.

"What if he wakes up?"

"Let him wake up," Susan says, beginning to moan. Her hips move back and forth.

"You're naughty," Chad says, smiling. He licks an areola.

Cars pass outside the window. Susan, with her top down, springs up and down over Chad. Martin does not wake up. Soon, Susan reaches the peak. She crumbles over Chad's body. But Chad has farther to go. He's still pushing. His movements take Susan up to the clouds again. She wraps her arms around his neck.

Chad finishes but stays inside. They hold each other in a warm embrace. Susan continues rocking softly back and forth.

"I think we should go to the lake," Susan says. "Tell my parents."

"I will go buy the ring tomorrow to make it official," Chad says.

"Will you propose to me again?"

"Hey, that's supposed to be a surprise!" Chad laughs.

"Ok. I can't wait for the surprise!" Susan replies.

As she drives to work, Susan hopes for a great future. She realizes how, working with the dead, this has so much meaning. Life is ephemeral. It passes by like a shooting star, even if not as quickly.

At the funeral home, she goes over the necessary paperwork and usual instructions relating her next patient, a young man who was beheaded, besides other details. Both the director and the owner of the facility step out for a moment. They have a meeting next door and leave her alone.

Susan finds beauty and service in her work, even if the circumstances that brought her patients to her were tragic. She does a good job, and is very respectful of the silent being upon the bed, as if he was only sleeping and she making sure he had a good rest before he woke up.

The cold hand to the back of her neck comes, abruptly, as she's thinking of Chad and applying the makeup to the dead man's eyes. She is powerless against such force, even after the bite comes and she tries to pull away with all her might. When she's discarded to the floor, all is dark. When she wakes up, the man sitting on the bed.

He sees her looking and answers her gaze, silently. Then he gets up, walking past her as if she was nothing.

Not long after he is gone, she hears the voices of the funeral director calling her. Susan is confused and scared. She rises to the ceiling to hide, and then floats into a door, into a dark room, from where she hears her name called more loudly, and the words,

"Where is she? Where is *he*?"

Full panic sets in, quickly.

With speed and concealment, Susan finds her way into the night. She is directionless, lost, confused. She hides from the people she thirsts. Though emptied terribly of blood, and her hunger almost getting the best of her, she is unable to leave her concealment.

Far in the fields, however, on the outskirts of Magnolias, she sees an opportunity. A lonely man with his dog on his way back home. Unable to stand her hunger any longer, she dives at full speed. With the man's face to the ground, she drinks as much as she can of his life, even as the dog barks and tears her dress with fangs and claws.

Almost flying with the dog clinging to her, she leaves the man. She has no pain from the dog's bites, except within her. The world is empty of an oasis for the dead. But she finds a solitary cabin far on a hill where she is able to rest in the day. While there, she thinks back without memory. Where did she come from? She knows she left something behind. But she knows the face of the one who brought her to this state. She's certain he gave her some poison. All she must do is wait, wait for clarity.

15

Waves break. Raven's Hill, a dark sea stack two miles offshore, rises a hundred feet above the water with its steep basalt face. Anika, Antonio, and Antonietta feel the cold spray. A full moon hangs in the north. Anika and Antonietta lean toward the center of their worlds, their hands resting on Antonio's shoulder. Their dresses flare and whip back like flames, as if the wind were a cold, sultry hand.

"See?" Antonio says. "This is something no mortal can live. Enjoy it, my loves. This is life-death. What gives us meaning."

There is a tall pole in the middle of the rock with a flickering light.

Even the dead marvel at the immensity of the ocean. Want to understand it. The sea is not afraid of them. It is master of all—of both the dead and the living. It cannot be opposed or challenged. All will lose. Antonietta, who ought not to fear anything but loneliness, feels awe as she gazes into the dark, impenetrable, seemingly infinite expanse.

The waves crash against the rock. The ocean lets it know it is coming. Time has already been gnawing at it, stripping it of its essence bit by bit. Antonietta looks up. The sky is full of stars.

"Oh, the sea has no enemies," Antonio says. "Though man with his luxuries makes safe haven for disease, she is too large for our small hands to destroy. See how pretty she is, and how powerful!"

Antonietta looks at him. She is strangely inspired by his words. She leans in and kisses his cheek. She lays a tender hand on his chest. She, who had not loved before, is now beginning to love, to be possessed. She is finally in the dream.

Anika looks at her from the other side. Though she feels secure in the knowledge that Antonio will never leave her, for death is an eternal marriage, her dead heart is alive with love and, like a stomach, it hates being the last to be served. She brings Antonio's face to her lips. Then she gazes back at the ocean and points.

Antonio looks beyond. "A ship sailing to Europe. Or maybe Africa."

"Oh, mighty seafarer!" Anika says. "You've got wings for the sea!"

Antonietta now looks at Anika. Anika feels her gaze and smiles. Antonietta seems to be inspired by her as well.

"I wonder what it would be like to live in the middle of these storms," Antonietta says; "on a ship that is sturdy in balance, and to come out every night when the moon is bright and the sea is peaceful."

"It is lonely," Antonio says. "Many people on that ship don't see their families a long time. In my old days, I knew a great hull named Majesty Isabella, an obscure ship at the time of the Black Ball Line, that traveled from New York to England in twenty-five days. All I wanted was to get home and play backgammon with my friends."

"I suppose you mean the three of us on that ship," Anika says to Antonietta. "And being the only ones there, as if we were the only souls in the world."

"There is beauty in being the only ones in the world," Antonietta says; "with somene on your side, especially among storms and swells, while we embrace and love, as if the earth was still."

Antonio looks at her, enchanted by her dreams. He strokes her cheek, and kisses her lips. "Perhaps we may one day." He holds Anika closer to him, and kisses her forehead. "But as to loving, who has ever made love upon this rock, so far from shore, with waves so angry that they sound like a thousand lions?" He looks into Anika's eyes. "You have been my love for a hundred years," he says. "The first kiss of my immortality. You've given life to this dead soul." He lays a caressing hand on her chin. "Your cold lips are a candle. Your flame gives me breath." He kisses her mouth. His other hand pulls Antonietta against him.

There is tugging and pulling, the raising of hems and the motion of hands, music from the scarlet lips, a pull of breath from breathlessness, the tactility warmed by blood. This heat in the blood exhales into the receiving mouths, gives animation to the fencing tongues, as the larynx of the ocean makes claim of the world, warns and embraces, and crashes angrily against the rock.

Clothes stay on since they are not spiritual and will fly away. Yet it doesn't take away from the nudity of passion and romance. Inhibition is shed with buttons on, all for the moon, and the moon keeps secrets. The women's legs go out of their center to receive between them the kiss of immortal love.

Antonietta has found her paradise, a paradise of fangs and love, of a desire she never lived before. She has drunk of the immortal saliva, its composition otherworldly and hypnotizing. It is this kiss, come with such substance, that makes mortals succumb to the bite when the goal to make them eternal begins with love. It promises rescue, or a salvation, and an eternal dream: a world of flowers where the long-fanged can saunter dreamily in their death, even after striking the living neck, the trough of spirits' nurture. After hunger has had its feed, and desire its fill, they wander in their dreamy death, with blood dripping from the tip of their fangs, and in company of each other, for one does not enjoy flowers alone in an eternal world.

Antonietta has already been in the garden. Antonio promised it, gave it, and now she eats of it through his lips.

What requires several visits to receive the gift of love, Antonietta obtained within her death. She has walked the dreamy path of the garden, and those walking with her are now her eternal companions and support. Her eternal lovers.

Albertini is now to compete, if he ever meets his enemies again, for the stolen fruit, the charmed fruit tenaciously hanging to this other branch from which she is afraid to fall.

And what if his arms are not enough? He is as inexperienced a vampire as a cub with promising fangs. What he was in life, could he be in death, regardless how much his company is missed? The land of darkness is another world. Yet one thing unites it with the daylight. What mortals seek in the day, vampires seek at nightfall: a cemented path, a firm path, a clear path.

As Albertini escapes the demons of his past, which in his mortal life were angels, and returns to the high tree within his little patch of woods, he looks beyond the stars and himself for direction.

He felt safe for a moment wandering the streets—as safe as a lion traversing Hyaenidae pawmarks past a curious cackle of hyenas—certain that his past would not haunt him in a familiar place—even as he was alive or refusing to believe he was dead.

When he finally thinks about it, he wonders what possessed him. The night before, he ran from his biped prey like a lion from an elephant, and then like a cub decided to test the waters and have a thrill among dangerous things, because after all he *is* a part of them, though he has fangs and claws, and a haughty certainty of his superior speed.

It was a miscalculated defiance added to a wrongheaded belief that he was immune from recognition because he showed his face. It was only when his past came back that he feared the world again, not so much because he saw his sister, but because she came to remind him that he was dead.

On the basalt rock, the three vampires make love. Their romantic tryst is not so secret. A wandering vampire, those who travel without consorts, lifted his gaze from below and saw them flying in direction of the sea. He recognized the central vampire and decided to follow.

He contemplates the scene from above now, the twisting bodies, the moving legs of the women, the moans of passion. After a moment, he returns to shore.

He looks around his environs, as if searching for something. He's suddenly by Albertini's woods. He hears a ruffle in the branches below.

"Bird or vampire?" he wonders.

At that moment, Albertini appears from the tree. The wandering vampire flies to him. He takes Albertini by the throat and hisses through his fangs like a cobra. Albertini's back crashes into the tree.

"You are new," says the wandering vampire.

Albertini stares with wonder at the glowing eyes.

"Are you afraid, lad?" the vampire asks.

Albertini does not answer.

"Ah, poor thing, just turned. What a fatality! They took out your tongue as well, so you wouldn't tell secrets."

It takes a moment for Albertini to regain his defiance.

"I would not do this, if I were you," he says, taking the vampire's wrist.

"Are you trying to fight me off?"

"No, keep your hand there," Albertini says, glancing quickly to the side. He is able to transmit danger. The vampire releases him. With the quickness of the dead, Albertini returns the favor. He seizes the vampire's throat and pins him against the same tree.

The vampire laughs.

"Let's be friends," he says.

"I don't think you know that word," Albertini says.

The vampire looks at him.

"I am Agnar," he says. "I am a wandering vampire, in search of friends and company."

"Your ways of acquiring them are a little odd," Albertini replies.

"I could not kill a vampire," Agnar says. "If you thought that, that means you are new, as I said before."

"I am a vampire, it seems. That's all that matters."

"I meant it when I said let's be friends," Agnar says. "You'll be safe. Let me go."

Albertini knows that clutching a vampire by the neck is useless work, unless you have a stake ready to bury in the heart. He releases Agnar. "Go," he says. "Leave me alone with my loneliness." He sits down against the tree.

Agnar looks at him. "Did you lose your company?" he asks.

"I thought you were going," Albertini says.

"I can't leave a soul in pain," Agnar says. "The dead cry louder than the living, and must be heard."

"I need no one to hear me," Albertini says.

"I'm all ears," Agnar replies.

Albertini looks at him, mystified.

"I lost a friend once, too," Agnar says. "And I cried louder than the living, because the pain of the dead is stronger. She was my Runa—my immortal love, done in by a mortal stake."

Agnar sits down next to Albertini and lays his hand on his forehead. He seems to suffer at the memory.

Albertini looks at him and then looks away. "Mine was taken by fangs, the same ones that turned me into a monster."

"Monster!" Agnar exclaims. "Monsters be the hills! They be the things that do not live. We are souls, wandering stars." He seems to have forgotten his suffering. "Oh, my dear Runa," he says afterward, remembering it again.

Though still a little angry, Albertini turns to him with curiosity. "What was she like?"

"She was a goddess of the night," Agnar says. "Two beautiful fangs adorned her mouth. Her sockets had oceans instead of eyes. Her hair was like the sun. Whenever she crossed the night, she seemed a shooting star."

Albrtini widens his yes. "Her hair was blond?"

"Yes," Agnar answers.

Albertini looks at the ground. "My girl had blond hair and blue eyes as well."

"You say the vampires that killed you also killed her?"

"Yes."

"Then she's also a vampire," Agnar says. "Unless they buried a stake in her."

Albertini looks at him again. Then he shakes his head. "No, I doubt it. They kidnapped her, I know. Antonio... He…"

"Antonio!" Agnar exclaims.

"Yes!" Albertini is surprised. "You know him?"

"Know him? I just saw him making love to two dead blondes on a large rock in the middle of the sea."

"Blondes!" Albertini exclaims. "Two of them?"

"I said two dead blondes. Damsels of the night. Two bright stars."

"One of them might... Making love, you say?"

"That's what I said," Agnar replies.

"It can't be. It could *not* be my Antonietta."

"You say she was blond as well?" Agnar asks.

"Yes."

"I see. Who knows? She might be the other lass. If she is, I'd wager she's his new companion. Vampires get consorts sometimes. It's how they adorn their existence."

Albertini can't contemplate it. A deep frown comes to his brow and he closes his eyes. Then he looks up. "It doesn't matter! I've returned! I will get back what is mine."

"If one of those blondes is your love, I suggest you forget her," Agnar says, simply.

Albertini is furious at this remark. "Forget her! Never!"

"Why try the impossible?" Agnar says. "I suspect that vampire is armed. And if he isn't, the women are. Vampire damsels carry wooden daggers in their purses. At least that's what they are to us. But they also carry makeup, which is another weapon—it raises the valor of the protective vampire, and makes him more dangerous. Ever since they invented mirrors with better backing, they use them profusely and to good advantage. If Antonio has made love to your goddess, she is no longer yours. She will die before losing him!”

“No! Stop! Your words anger me! You do not wish friendship! She would never leave me!”

Agnar is not dissuaded. “Don’t compare life with death,” he says. “She met you in life, she met Antonio in death. Two worlds. Even if she remembers you, she might not wish to part from what she knows.”

“She doesn’t know him!”

“How quickly did she die?”

“Does it matter?” Albertini almost yells—though, without knowing how to proceed, he doesn’t move.

“Yes,” Agnar says. “If she died slowly, there is no hope. If quickly, you might have a chance—unless she’s walked in the Dream, the one that all the dead know.”

Albertini doesn’t know about this “Dream,” and it means nothing to him. “Where do I find him?” he asks. “Where is that rock?”

Agnar, however, knows the importance of the Dream, the one that all the dead know—or *should* know, like Albertini. It is the vampires’ marriage of their souls to each other. “You are going to fight three vampires?” he exclaims, for he is including Antonietta among the foes.

“No, only two,” Albertini says.

Agnar looks at Albertini with surprise. He wants to laugh, but doesn’t.

“I would help you,” he says, leaning back. “But unfortunately I am tired tonight. Might sleep all day tomorrow. But, if you insist, you should go prepared.” He digs into his jacket and pulls out a stake. “They carry these, and among three, they’d be hard-pressed to miss. Bury it in Antonio’s heart, keep the women and come meet me here. If they keep you alive, that is.”

Albertini stands and takes the stake. “I will return with his heart!—and his head!”

“Interesting!” Agnar says. “But make sure the stake stays in his body. I’ve never killed a vampire, not one already wandering around, at least, and I suspect ancient vampires are stronger than most.”

Albertini nods and asks for the location of the rock.

“Over yonder that way,” Agnar says. “He might still be there, making love to his two women.”

Albertini rises to the sky and flies in direction of the rock.

16

By the time Albertini arrives at Raven's Hill, the three lovers are gone. He returns to the woods where Agnar is waiting for him.

"Don't worry, tomorrow is another night," Agnar says.

Albertini sits down against the tree without replying.

"You have many nights," Agnar continues. "Eternity is long. If you're so certain you can steal back your lass tonight, you should be able to do it tomorrow, or anytime." Agnar, despite his twenty-year-old appearance, is a long-lived vampire who understands patience and the difference between mortal and immortal lives.

Albertini leans his head back against the tree and closes his eyes.

"What about a drink?" Agnar says. "That will make you feel better. Mortals are enjoyable company, as long as you keep your fangs off your neighborhood."

Albertini looks at Agnar.

"Yes," Agnar says. "Your neighborhood should not be your hunting ground. Also, it should not be the town where you grew up—people will recognize you, and… that can be as dangerous as the sun, if not worse."

"You mean, go somewhere else?"

"Yes, at least a hundred miles, where people did not know you in life. Even if someone recognized you, you could always say they are mistaken. Make your new town your new backyard, don't pee in it."

"I understand," Albertini replies. He holds his head, still depressed.

Twenty miles away, in a cabin on a lonely hill, is the girl Albertini transformed. Susan still remembers him. The hill and the cabin are a great place to hide—a propitious discovery. It is far enough for humanity to be scarce and the area too uninteresting for anyone to care about.

Susan sleeps in the closet, where she is protected from the murderous sunlight. There, she tries to place herself in her new world, trying to understand it and her new self.

As the days go by—both for her and Albertini—she begins to recall the fragments of her life. Chad, her fiancé, comes back as a painful blast. To realize you're a new being, banished from sunlight and your old society, and thrust into a state of loneliness, is a painful price to pay for the momentary hunger of an immortal monster.

Susan only wakes up to remember. The blood she drank from the jogger with his dog will keep her strong for a couple of weeks before her next hunger. This is the reality for most vampires, except for those with an opportunity for love. Being near blood makes you lusty for passion, and that makes your fangs sprout from your maxilla even if you're well-fed. Love is a dessert on the vampire's table. Even when you're full, you might as well have that, because it is sweet.

Susan's full memory does not return. As for most new vampires, it returns in patches, and many things are forgotten. Yet the few things she *does* remember are enough to make her feel deep resentment for the man on the mortuary bed. She knows he did something to make her feel different. At the very least, she wants answers—wants to know what he put in the drink of her life that changed her, irrevocably. Taking the life of the jogger gave her part of the answer. This is what Albertini did. They were alone. Her body was there to violate, and he violated it. Now she is alone, without society, without love! The white wedding—that was not too far away—will no longer be wearing a dress.

On the other hand, the passing days, rather nights, have strengthened Antonietta's bond with her companions. It's almost as if she has forgotten her mortal past, or chooses to forget it, because it lacked *this*, this undefinable thing that defines her now. The bond between the three is almost exclusive. That keeps the sociable necks—the flirts and debonairs—safe from their "romantic fangs." Having each other to satisfy their need of love, Anika, Antonio and Antonietta hunt only out of hunger.

Joanna is shocked as the trio makes love right in front of her. She glances at Engusanado with wide, rounded eyes. Engusanado, for his part, only yawns at the scene, as if tired. For Joanna, this consummates her resentment toward her blistered hands and face, and toward Engusanado. Not long after their love making, the nude trio is ready for more adveture. Antonietta goes into the suitcase and pulls out a shirt and a mini skirt. Anika selects similar items to match her. Antonio dons the same pants and jacket. Anika gives Antonietta a new hair-do—it is simple, just a few clips here and there to pick up her hair—and traces red lipstick on her lips. It is only ten o'clock when the three leave the crypt.

Still satiated since a week ago, blood is not a need. They have some money to spend from some thefts in town, and arrive at Magnolias. Antonietta seems like a different woman with her new but simple hair-do and even her new confidence, and eyes that might recognize her are overlooking her or are absent. The trio enters a bar.

"This drink has life," Antonio says, looking at his glass filled with Old Fashioned. "It reminds me of the good ol' Sazerac I drank in my youth."

"I've heard of that," says the bartender.

"Have you, my lad?" Antonio asks.

The bartender laughs at the address.

"Yes, sir-lad," he replies with humor. "It's an old drink. My father is a connoisseur of old cocktails. He has a big book of historical drinks."

"Very interesting," Antonio replies. "Is that why you chose your trade?"

"My trade? You mean bartending? You could say that. I learned to mix drinks early on."

"You're not a vampire, are you?"

The bartender laughs. "I know why you ask. There are people in town who like to dress like Dracula. I'm too old for that."

Anika and Antonietta look with curiosity at the bartender and smile at each other. It's a unique smile—one that, if their lips were slightly parted, might look like laughter.

"Where do you guys hail from?" The bartender asks, suddenly. He's evidently attracted to Anika and Antonietta.

"We, my good sir, are from another time," Antonio says.

Now the girls laugh.

"Maybe you should come visit one day," Antonio says.

The bartender laughs, too. "I'm too busy to go to another time. Unless it's around the block." He wants to keep composure, but the joke offends him a little. "No, really, are you guys from out of town?"

"Yes, but not too far," Antonio replies.

"I see."

The bartender realizes that Antonio is the party's voice and that he will get nothing from the girls.

He is a little mistaken. Antonietta and Anika have been resting their fingers on their cheeks, contemplative and admiring. Anika turns to Antonio. Her eyes seem to focus on him and the bartender.

"It's your dream," Antonio says, understanding that glance.

Anika leans over the bar. "Excuse me?"

"Yes?" the bartender turns from his glasses. He is already enchanted. He never heard a voice so sweet, saw a smile so beautiful, swam in eyes so shiny. He smiles, broadly.

"What is your name?" Anika asks.

"My name?" He looks at Antonio, who smiles at him. "I'm Orland," he says to Anika. "And you?"

"I will tell you," Anika says. "But you must come with me."

Orland raises his eyebrows with surprise. "Come with you?"

Anika calls him close with her finger. Orland leans over.

Anika whispers in his ears. "I want you."

Orland looks at Antonio. Antonio raises his glass.

Orland, familiar with the establishment, takes Anika through a dark passage into a bathroom that is out of service.

Half an hour later, Anika returns, adjusting her skirt.

Orland gets censured by the other bartender and wondering glances from the busboys. Orland has nothing to fret about. He only smiles. His hypnosis didn't take away his memory. It simply raised his temperature to the point he couldn't say no. He gives Anika, Antonio, and Antonietta free a drink. He hands Anika his phone number. Anika puts it in her top.

After the drinks and a little chat, Antonio, Anika, and Antonietta depart.

17

Nigh the stars, a creature watching. Dark heaven is Albertini's lookout post. He sees three figures in the air. Their swift flight is relaxed and full of laughter. Their voices infuriate him—sounds of joy are a dagger to lonesome spirits. He doesn't know who they are, only that they anger him. They sound like spoiled teenage immortals flying home from some little fun-filled trip down at the lake.

Yet they could be the vampires he's after. He lets them fly for a moment before following them. He doesn't feel safe approaching them, just like a lion would not feel safe taking on three buffaloes alone. Cautioned by Agnar's words, and despite his pride, he counts Antonietta as one of the buffaloes. She might have changed after all and want nothing to do with him. Perhaps she might not remember him.

That would be a bitter feeling. He hopes that she will see him and fly back to him. He'll cast the stake to the ground, forgive Antonio and Anika, and let them go on their way as he flies into the night, holding Antonietta's hand, her head on his shoulder, with love reborn or a love that never died. Forgiveness will be his new weapon and shield.

The thought gives him faster wings. He'll allow the buffaloes to retreat to their grass, as they leave him to his own, because there will be enough savannah for everyone. One must just convince the buffaloes of that, especially when one is the lion.

The trio seems to dip into the darkness as into water as they fly—because as they do so, they disappear. Suddenly, they reappear, which is confusing to Albertini. When they disappear again, Albertini sees them no more. He arrives near the point where he last saw them and goes down. His descent lands him behind the gate of a desolate cemetery. There are trees, wild grass and flowers, graves, and mausoleums. He looks right and left. He does not know what to do or where to go, even if he knew what to do. He just stands behind the gate, hoping they will reappear and that he can see his Antonietta.

After some moments, he hears voices. He sees three vampires take to the air.

"That's my Antonietta!" he exclaims. "I know you as I know the stars." Then, thinking of Antonio, he frowns. "Oh, that beast has had you!" He takes to the air.

Antonietta does not even sense him. She is flying in the dream, in the garden. She disappears within the air as within water, and then resurfaces as if for a glance at the moon. Antonio and Anika themselves appear and disappear, like swimmers of the air, sinking and rising again.

They land on the top floor of Magnolias Hotel. The women have purses with them. In them they carry money, cigarettes, and protection against enemy vampires, plus makeup. Things a damsel of the night needs.

The upper part of the hotel is normally open, but tonight it is closed. It is furnished with couches and umbrellas, a bar, and a thick glass wall that goes around, offering a view of the city. Construction tools are scattered, as if the roof is being fixed or redesigned. Cement bag, buckets, paintbrushes, and shovels abound. Amidst all this, a large Jacuzzi bubbles peacefully, catching the diamond glows of the moon. The lovers don't pay attention to any of this. As they materialize, they want more of the dream. It comes through hands and kisses. Anika and Antonietta are back in their typical dresses: Anika in her red dress, Antonietta in her black.

The lovers come together against one point of the wall. Antonio's hands busy themselves with bringing joy to both women, who kiss their moans into each other's mouths.

Soon, their hands are on the center of his body. Antonio kisses Antonietta's neck.

To a random onlooker, the figures would appear and disappear, and make him think he's dreaming.

Albertini can't see them, even though he is perched on the wall and is looking around. He lost them on the way and came here to curse the unforgiving fate that allowed him to lose his Antonietta once again. But then, the passionate figures reappear. Albertini is looking in the right direction when it happens. He recognizes his love. His Antonietta.

"Antonietta!" he cries loudly, angry that he saw what he just saw—his love sharing her undead moist with those who tore her from his life.

Antonio and the women stop. Antonietta looks his way.

Albertini descends. His blue eyes glow red with anger. He takes two steps toward the trio and stops.

"Have you become a harlot!" he exclaims, unable to help himself. He is angry. Jealous. More than tha—the stake of rage is buried in his heart.

"Well, look who came out of his grave!" Antonio says, his fangs already threatening.

Albertini remembers his new weapon. "No!" he exclaims. He puts up a palm. "Stay away! You are not a threat to me. I'm not here to fight. Let bygones be bygones. What happened in life will stay in life, what happens in death, in death."

"You have become a philosopher," Antonio says. "If that is the case, what do you seek? This is life no more, this is death."

"I came here to get back what is mine," Albertini says.

"Yours? Since when does death own slaves? Death is a liberator, unless you are a zombie who walks as if with a heavy burden. Unfortunately, they must find their own way. Everyone else does as he pleases." He looks at Antonietta. "Or as *she* pleases."

Albertini also looks at Antonietta. He extends his hand.

"I've been wandering the world of death looking for you," he says. "I will be the slave, slave to the one who possessed me in life."

Antonio crosses his arms and nods, impressed by the poetry.

Antonietta looks at Albertini.

"Your words are beautiful," she says. "But so is my dream. Unless you have a garden like the one I have found, there is no path for us. Why should I toss all my jewels for an uncertain eternity with you?"

Albertini is shocked. Antonietta did not come to him. Anika observes Albertini. Albertini feels her glance. He points at her.

"*She* is you killer! The one you have been sharing your love with, your dream. The dream you feel, it should be mine!"

"Me? A killer?" Anika responds, a little offended. "You forget that you lied to us. I would have gone to my usual prey had you told us the truth about your little game. Pretending to be a vampire. Your neck was not very appealing. Except for Antonietta, you had not much going for yourself."

Antonio almost laughs.

Albertini almost reaches for the stake inside his jacket, insulted at Antonio's little laugh. He suddenly steps forward again.

"You are coming with me," he says to Antonietta.

Antonio gets in front of his new lover, though he is still distant.

Albertini pauses. "Get out of my way, or I'll strike you with my stake!"

All this time, Anika hasn't let go of her purse. It has been hanging on her arm. She pulls out her own stake.

"You mean like this one?" she says. "You think we vampires don't know our dangers? These are as much our enemies as our friends."

Albertini suddenly feels in danger. But he is defiant.

"You are coming with me!" he says to Antonietta. "I'll show you a better dream." He walks a little more, though now with more caution.

"Wait!" Anika says. "If you want her to go with you, she has to accept." She stretches her hand to Antonietta. Antonietta takes it. "Do you wish to go with him?" she asks.

Antonietta, holding Anika's hand, looks at Albertini. Then she glances at Anika. Then at Antonio. Both her companions smile. She looks at Albertini again. Without releasing Anika's hand, she steps back.

"I'm sorry, I can't," she says.

"They have poisoned you!" Albertini says.

"I have drunk of a dream," Antonietta says. "My spirit has found a home, even if the dream is poison."

Albertini is so angry now, that even as Anika holds her own stake, he flies to her. But Antonio is not a statue. As Albertini takes a leap, the quick vampire blocks him.

Albertini crashes against the wall. That makes him start digging for his stake. Anika, however, is ready with hers. Letting go of Antonietta's hand, she's quickly on him. She knows that an angry vampire is hard to contain and must be disposed of.

Antonio, ever observant, also flies to Albertini. Anika is ready to bury her stake into the rebel vampire, but Albertini, himself now a quick spirit, eludes Antonio's efforts, lunging forward before a solid grasp can be made on his arms, and falls on top of her.

But Albertini has more than one enemy. Somewhere in the night, a woman has been wandering around, angry at him—Susan, who recognizes him.

If the ire for losing your girlfriend in life is strong, there is nothing like the rage of a woman ripped from her wedding night. Claws of hell descend upon Albertini's neck and face, accompanied by a wild, piercing shriek in his ears.

As she rips into Albertini's face with pure vengeance, Antonio pulls him off Anika's body and, with the help of the newcomer—who never lets go of her prey—pins him onto his back. Susan serves as an anchor against his escape. At last, the stake is buried! Albertini feels it. Yet the abrupt sound from his mouth is not from pain, nor the sudden glow in his eyes from looking at the place he is entering—it is from the face of the one who delivered the blow—Antonietta!

Albertini reaches for her. "Why?"

"This is my dream!" Antonietta says.

As Albertini looks at the one who was his love in life, Antonietta retreats and turns.

"This time, you won't live," Antonio says. He pushes the stake even deeper into Albertini's heart.

As Antonio finishes the job, Antonietta, looking away, becomes suddenly immobile. Her hands go to her mouth.

Antonio looks at her and follows the direction of her eyes. Anika has a stake in her heart.

"No!" he cries. He flies quickly to her, pulls out the stake, and sends it crashing into the wall.

"Oh, my precious goddess," he says, kneeling, holding her dear, cold hand.

"I have lived a great death," Anika says. "The garden disappears. I am now mortal. I see my past. I can see the sun in her full glory. I am not afraid anymore. I'm going back. My love is reaching for me. I am going."

Antonio leans forward and kisses her.

Antonietta also kneels, her hands on her chest. She seems to pray as Anika's open eyes freeze upon the stars and the moon. Her hands close Anika's eyes.

"Oh, beautiful goddess," Antonio says. "The night won't be the same without you. I will live it in your honor." He looks at the stake he cast to the wall and rushes to it. He returns to Albertini and stabs the lad a thousand times. But this is revenge against the dead. Albertini's spirit has already left his body.

Antonio tosses aside the stake and returns to Anika.

"Oh, my lovely queen!" he says, kneeling again. "Say one last word, oh dear night star, say one last word!" He closes his eyes and bows his head. Then he strokes Anika's hair. "I will live your dream. I will never be alone as long as you are in my memory." He looks at Antonietta, who is standing now, touching his back. "Come, we must take the angel to her resting place." He stands up and looks down. Antonietta leans her hand on his shoulder.

Susan is on the floor, looking at him and Antonietta. She seems a little confused and a little scared. "You are alone," Antonio says to her and smiles. "Come with us." He stretches out his hand.

Susan looks at both vampires a moment. She takes Antonio's hand.

Antonio puts Susan's hand in Antonietta's. "Your new sister," he says, then he turns to Susan. "From now on, you won't be alone." He kneels and, with undead strength, takes Anika's body in his arms. "We must be quick, but also loving," he says.

They fly into the sky. Antonio carries Anika with tenderness. They arrive at the mausoleum. Susan and Antonietta walk in holding hands. Antonio carries Anika solemnly down the steps to the crypt. Antonietta raises the lid of the casket and bows as Antonio lays Anika in her old bed.

"Rest now, dear goddess," Antonio says.

Engusanado is in his hole next to Joanna, a burning candle outside. Antonio approaches him and, without waking him, reaches into the breast pocket of his old jacket, which Engusanado is still wearing. When he returns to Anika, he takes her hand and slips her old ring on her finger.

"Go back to him," he says; then looks up. "William, she is yours. She was never mine." He looks at Anika again. "Oh, dear goddess. You are back now. Back home. This was just a pit stop of your spirit on the way to your love—the one truly yours. I'm glad you stopped by. What you were in death—a light in the darkness—you'll be in your new paradise. Your light will dim Heaven's light."

He finds the stem of the old rose Anika had held against her breast. It no longer has the rose, or even a petal, but he places the stem under her hands, against her chest. Slowly, Anika becomes merely cheekbones, mandible, frontal bone, and empty eye-sockets.

"Go to your beloved," he says. "Remember me, if you will. Or if not—if this should be a nightmare to you—remember the old life, when you sprinted wildly over the hills as a happy child. May your spirit have a happy existence, oh beautiful one! Goodbye!"

He lowers the lid onto the casket and looks at Antonietta.

"This is home no more," he says. "Too many dear memories in this place, made bitter by her quiet presence." He looks toward Engusanado. "You old man, take care. Be as happy as you can be. Keep the jacket."

Susan looks at him in a new light. She recognizes a noble and loving spirit.

Antonio smiles at her. "Let not this adventure darken your spirit. We will find solace together"—he looks at Antonietta— "and with each other. Let us go, my goddesses. Into the night. I know another place where we can go for a little while, while we find a new home. It may be a castle this time. Come."

He grabs the suitcase and walks up the steps, holding Antonietta— his foremost companion now—by the hand.

Engusanado heard everything. He sits up as Antonio makes his way up the steps.

"Goodbye, friends," he says, waving his bony hand. He approaches Anika's casket. He is able to pull up the lid, though he doesn't open it all the way. "Oh!" he exclaims. "This is a tragedy. Antonio has left with the new woman. This is Anika. Oh, who will put the earth back on me now? I have no more friends."

He puts down the lid again and looks toward his grave. Joanna is sleeping.

"Oh, I do not love you!" he says. "And yet, you are my only company now. We must do what we can. That is what marriage is. At least when both people are alone."

He goes up the steps and out of the mausoleum into the garden. The red rose seems more vibrant than ever. "Oh, you rose," Engusanado says. "You are now the only life in this cemetery." He looks up and around. The vampires, who were his friends, have now abandoned him. He walks around the garden and hunts for worms.

18

Engusanado doesn't hunt worms for long. He sits on his bony heels—heels slightly covered with his old skin—and bends over with existential pain.

"Oh, undo the spell!" he says, almost as if he would cry. "What must the dead do to die? What is my punishment? Is that for the time I took my brother's bicycle without permission and did not apologize? Or is it my bad decisions in business and in love? Was it my impure thoughts after church? What must the dead do to die?"

As he sits, he begins to feel tired, very tired.

"Oh, I feel more tired than I ever did," he says. "I should go to bed."

He gets up and returns to the crypt. Joanna is awake.

"Did you bring some worms?" she asks.

"I am too tired," he says, walking toward her.

Joanna sighs an old breath, crosses her arms, and gets out of the hole.

"Well, if you must sleep, I'll make room. Once again, I must do everything myself! You could have brought a worm or two, at least? Even dead you won't do the bare minimum!"

Engusanado has only eyes for the hole this time. When he gets near, he collapses and falls in. Joanna is surprised.

"He must be very tired," she says. "For someone who is dead, very tired. I guess I must do the hunting now."

Yet she hardly takes a step when she falls to the ground. She dies, completely.

Engusanado had never learned the secret. All his dead life, only a half-death, he had lived suffering, always thinking, always attached to memories. When those memories went away, he wanted to make a new life in death, as if he was alive. Upon realizing the waste of his death, that he had nothing more to live for—and uttering a desire to finally quit—the spell broke. With his end, Joanna's end also came, since it was he who gave her life.

Next morning, John Alexios and Abel Mathias enter the mausoleum along with workers. They can't believe what they see in the crypt. They see Joanna on the floor and Engusanado in his hole. Old cemetery Records show one of the caskets is empty. The discovery quickly becomes national news, and the media cover it, ceaselessly.

"The body of Joanna Riddler found in an old, abandoned mausoleum on the outskirts of Magnolias," the news reports go. *"Forensic analysts will study the bones of the man in the uncovered shallow grave."*

With so many strange things occurring, people are beginning to wonder if there is more to the world than meets the eye.

Roselin certainly thinks so. She has met someone new on the streets of Magnolias, and man named Agnar, with whom she discusses the latest events. They are walking together down Magnolia's Blvd.

"Too many strange things happening," she says.

"Too many, indeed," Agnar agrees.

"But back to the point, you say you were a friend of Albertini?"

"Yes," Agnar says. "It's strange what happened. I don't mean to bring bad memories."

"I've been too shocked to be shocked anymore," Roselin says. "I no longer know if to be pissed or sad. Not until I learn more. My parents want me to grieve like a respectable woman, but when you see your dead brother walking down the street smoking a cigarette…I don't know what to think. I refuse to be unhappy that he's dead, when he…but he *did* go away really fast. I don't know what to think!"

"You say he was, or is, a vampire?" Agnar asks. "I didn't know that about him."

"Yes, he was. A real one," Roselin says.

"So you are used to vampires, then?" Agnar asks.

"More used to them than to college. He never took me, or has taken me—I don't fucking *know* what to say anymore!—to any of his parties.

I've always wanted to know what the vampire world is like."

"Interesting," Agnar says. "I can show you."

"No way! You are a vampire?" Roselin is surprised.

"Shh, tell no secrets," Agnar says.

"Will you show me what a vampire is?"

"With pleasure! I wouldn't be a gentleman if I didn't show a lady what a vampire is. But we need a quiet place. People around here are too...superstitious."

Roselin laughs. She trusts Agnar. He is a young man with charming eyes and a *no-do-wrong kind of vibe*. He is also handsome, confident, and funny. It is possible that he is not very moral, but that is part of the thrill. If he doesn't show her what a vampire is, he might help her forget *all the BS* at home and in town.

Not far from them is Magnolias' Hotel. The stake is still in Albertini's body on the top floor, where no one has yet shown up to do even a bit of cleaning.

Twenty miles away there's a cemetery, and in it a mausoleum that, like the one John Alexios discovered, also seems to have been abandoned by people and time.

Antonio is with Antonietta and Susan. They appear out of the mausoleum.

"She will always be with us," Antonio says to Antonietta and Susan, holding both women by the waist. "We will honor her in the most memorable way." He looks at both of them. "My goddesses, let us visit the stars!"

They fly high into the sky, past many clouds, till below the world, maybe the earth is almost gone. The winds are wild. They push and raise the women's dresses. Antonio kisses Antonietta and Susan, and lowers himself between their legs. The women share of the dream, the hypnotic saliva, singing the hymn of their love in each other's mouth.

In this dream, Antonietta and Antonio remember Anika, still a star shining in their world, while Susan, for the first time in her life, drinks the drink of immortal love.

THE END

Antonio and Anika—a walk in Magnolias

AFTERWORD

This is the second edition to "The Passion of the Immortals." Where is the first? Well, it was never really distributed, and, based on the rules of the publisher, I could not submit new files since the first was, in its esteem, "published." It was also written under a pen name I no longer care for.

This second edition is not a rewrite of the story of Anika and Antonio, but rather a cleanup job, with the addition of a new chapter which I felt was somewhat important to understand the characters "a little better." This is the chapter of the bar, where the characters demonstrate that "blood" is not always the end. Not adding that new chapter would not have, perhaps, made much of a difference, but I found it somewhat important to include. It rather, I believe, added than deducted from the story. Other than that, no new major characters were introduced, just an event.

I hope, with all my heart, that you enjoy your little stroll down dark passion's garden, get a little scared, a little excited, and have sweet, Gothic-moonlit dreams.

— Maxime Norrvik, Friday Dec 20, 2024, Los Angeles CA.

About the Author

Maxime Norrvik is a writer from Los Angeles. An ex-student of Journalism, Mr. Norrvik has been writing since a very young age. While he has written several manuscripts, he considers himself a musician first and a writer second. He has lived in Australia where he has a daughter, Sephil, named after a characters in one of his stories.

He is the author of *The Passion of the Immortals, the Passion of Adelia* and the forthcoming novel *Other Gods*. His favorite Gothic novel is *Dracula*, from Bram Stoker. He's also a fan of Alexander Dumas, Victor Hugo, George Eliot, Jane Austen and other classic and contemporary authors' stories—too many to count.

Maxime Norrvik's works invite readers to take a stroll down existentialism's lane, where the extraordinary feels tangible and the mundane and magical brim with truth and philosophical pondering.